The Sons of Some Dear Mother

The five sons of Dorothy Daniels – Frank, a notorious gunman; Hugh, an attorney; Urban, a drifter who works odd jobs; Virgil, a sober and serious rancher; and the youngest, Casey – reunite in their hometown of Blue Springs Creek, Missouri, for their mother's funeral, after she is murdered.

The townspeople are shocked, and an eyewitness claims it was the outlaw leader Henry Lowe and the Murdock Gang who were responsible. When the brothers become disillusioned with the local law and their lack of pursuit, they decide to track down the gang themselves and get their vengeance.

On the trail of the murderous outlaws, the brothers start to find some of the brotherly love they had lost since they were kids. The trail is filled with danger, duels and death. The brothers will risk everything to get justice for their mother – especially Frank, the toughest and most ruthless of Dorothy's sons.

The Sons of Some Dear Mother

Matt Cole

A Black Horse Western

ROBERT HALE

© Matt Cole 2019
First published in Great Britain 2019

ISBN 978-0-7198-3007-5

The Crowood Press
The Stable Block
Crowood Lane
Ramsbury
Marlborough
Wiltshire SN8 2HR

www.bhwesterns.com

Robert Hale is an imprint
of The Crowood Press

Typeset by
Derek Doyle & Associates, Shaw Heath
Printed and bound in Great Britain by
4Bind Ltd, Stevenage, SG1 2XT

'Men are what their mothers made them.'

Ralph Waldo Emerson

'Sons are the anchors of a mother's life.'

Sophocles

'There has never been, nor will there ever be, anything quite so special as the love between a mother and a son.'

Unknown

CHAPTER 1

SOME KIND OF GOD

There was an ugly word that maybe the preacher, the Reverend Elston Hagwood, officiating at the funeral, had not used as yet. That word was murdered! But it was uppermost in the thoughts of every man, woman and child standing in the Missouri rain that awful day. It was bad enough that the most respected matriarch in the county was dead, but the fact that she had been mercilessly gunned down by outlaw scum unfit to breathe the same air as her was intolerable.

'Dear Lord, we come today to honor our loved one. We are gathered here today, not only to grieve the loss of Dorothy Daniels, but also to give thanks to you for her life among us. We are gathered here today, not only to mourn over how different our lives will be without her, but also to give thanks to you for how full life was when she was with us. We have gathered here today, not only to consider the shortness

7

and uncertainty of life on earth, but also to give thanks to you for the gift of life and the gift of family and the gift of friendships. Lord, we ask that you would comfort us this day as we come together to share love and sweet memories with one another,' the Reverend Hagwood said, then paused. 'In Jesus' name we pray, amen.'

The preacher's voice was steady and unemotional. Although as outraged as anybody, he was not about to inflame already raw emotions by playing up to the popular sentiment. He meant to lay Dorothy Daniels next to her late husband, Isaac, with full ceremony and dignity, as befitted the life she had led in Clay County. There would be no talk of hatred or revenge in his eulogy; there was enough of that everyplace else, without his adding to it.

The whole town was there to honor one of the last of the county's genuine pioneers, and to support her sons in their time of sorrow.

Married for forty-one years, up to the time of Isaac Daniels' death a few years before, the Daniels had produced five strapping sons. Four of them were at the funeral, and they made an impressive if heart-breaking sight, standing tall and dark-suited in line as the casket was slowly lowered into the grave along-side their father.

Hugh, the eldest of the four present, had arrived the previous day from Kansas where he had a thriving law practice. Young Casey, only twenty years of age as of last week had shown what he was made of by taking charge of the arrangements after the brutal shock of learning of his mother's murder. Virgil, the sober and serious rancher, had to be restrained from going after the killers before the burial. Urban, the drifter, had reached town just that morning by train from St Louis.

Few people had ever been given a more impressive farewell than the Daniels – Isaac first, and now Dorothy – but something was missing. And everybody knew what it was – or more accurately, who it was: Frank Daniels.

The brothers tried every way they knew to contact big Frank, while Missouri newspapers made front page stories of the senseless murder of Dorothy Daniels at the hands of the Murdock Gang. Wires had been dispatched to places he was known to visit, places as far apart as El Robles, Mexico, to Indian Knife, Canada.

It was more than a year since Clay County had laid eyes on giant Frank Daniels, but nobody ever forgot him. He had always been like that, a man who could make a lifetime impression just by saying 'howdy'.

It made folks sadder still to think of Frank Daniels missing out on his mother's burial. With one thing and another, there was hardly a dry eye in the Blue Springs Creek graveyard as the good reverend summed up what it was all about.

'Her life was a good life . . . the sons of some dear mother . . . she is our loss if the good Lord's gain.'

The rain continued to hiss down harder than ever. Hugh, as the oldest son present, was handed the shovel to send down the first clay clods.

As he dug the blade into the earth, he seemed to freeze. Then he turned his head sharply and stared at his brothers, as though somebody had spoken. Three solemn faces told him otherwise. The Reverend Hagwood cleared his throat. Something had distracted Hugh from his solemn task, all right. He straightened up and looked around until his eyes fixed on the ridge behind the cemetery.

It wanted an hour or two of sunset on a lovely evening as a single horseman made his way eastwards, across the high dry prairie land between the upper portion of the river and the trail that led into town. He was a big man, of great personal power, a figure that promised great agility and the capability of enduring fatigue; most remarkable was the shadow that he cast.

On the croup of his horse, attached to the cantle of the saddle, he carried a small valise of untanned leather, with a superb Mexican blanket of blue and scarlet strapped upon it, and a large leather bottle with a horn drinking cup swinging from it on one side; on the other was fastened a portion of the loin of a fat buck, which had fallen in the course of the morning by his rifle.

The horse that carried this well-appointed rider was a dark brown thoroughbred.

At length, when the sun was no longer above three times the width of its own disc from the level line of the lowest plain, he set spur to his horse, and pushed him on from the raking trot he had hitherto maintained into a long swinging gallop, which carried him over the ground at a good rate.

After he had ridden at this pace for twenty or thirty minutes, he reached the brow of one of the low, rolling waves of earth that constitute the surface of the prairie; from here the land fell away in a long gentle slope for some six or seven miles towards the east, and the experienced eye of the horseman could make out a heavy growth of timber – this he knew was the deep forest of his youth, within its shadowy depths a wide and never failing river that he used to fish with his father and brothers. A short hour brought him closer to the forest – and closer to home – just as the sun was setting.

Through this wild paradise the mighty river rolled its pellucid waves, rapid and strong, and as transparent as the purest crystal.

Galloping his horse joyously over the rich green turf, the traveler soon reached the river, to a spot where it was bordered by a little breach or margin of pure white sand, almost as hard as marble; and wading into the cool, clear water till it washed the heaving flanks of his thoroughbred, he let it drink long and deep of the pure beverage, water having not touched its thirsty lips since the early morning.

This duty done, he returned to the shore – he was running late – in order to make his way to something he did not wish to attend. Selecting an oak tree about two feet in girth, around which the grass grew tall and luxuriant, he tied his horse to its trunk with his lasso – a cord of plaited hide – that he kept coiled at his saddle bow.

After polishing his accoutrements as if for a parade – though this was not a day of joy for him – he checked his saddle-bags to ensure they were secure. Satisfied that everything was fine, he reluctantly climbed back on to his horse, and with a slight nudge urged the animal onwards. He could see the town's edge – a familiar sight for him, though it had been a long time since he had seen it – as he rode. He paused before topping the ridge, as he knew those in town would see him as soon as he did.

Frank Daniels took in a deep breath, let it out slowly, and checked if his tears were still coming. They were gone now.

With that he topped the ridge.

Above the puzzled murmur of adult voices, a child cried: 'There's someone up there, Mommy!'

Every person, no matter what their age, turned to the ridge. And there they could see the dark silhouette of a man beside his horse, veiled but not hidden by the deluge of rain. The man appeared very big, and to at least one of the Daniels brothers, he looked very familiar.

The shovel slipped from Hugh's hands as his eyes widened.

'It's Frank,' he whispered. Then, because nobody had heard, he shouted it: 'It's our brother Frank!'

Scarcely anyone seemed ready to believe him until the tall figure started down from the top of the ridge.

There could be no mistaking that distinctive, arm-swinging walk.

'Yeah!' breathed Urban Daniels. 'It is him all right! He made it!'

For some reason, people began to applaud and cheer, the way folks do at a theater when things are going badly and the hero makes his entrance.

Until that moment, everything had been unrelievedly bad: the murder, the grief, the sense of affront and outrage to an entire community, even the appalling weather for the funeral. But the eleventh-hour arrival of big Frank Daniels, the eldest of the sons of Dorothy and Isaac Daniels, seemed to put things in a different perspective, and to offer some relief and hope just when people needed it the most.

At least one man there, a grizzled old veteran who had cowboyed for the Daniels for near twenty-five years, saw something more in Frank's arrival.

'This is what we wanted,' he confided to those around him as the Daniels broke into a run to welcome their brother. 'They're done for now, and that's for sure.'

'Who?' someone asked with a frown.

'The killers, of course. That giant Frank will be wearin' their guts for gaiters inside a week, I reckon.' The cowboy slapped his thigh and smiled for the first time since the awful killing. 'By Glory, this is the best thing that could have happened. I would rather have Old Scratch hisself on my tail than big Frank Daniels.'

His listener, a newcomer to Blue Springs Creek,

thought that the cowboy might be overstating the case. Those who knew Frank, either personally or by legend, sided with the cowboy.

'Why, Marlene,' the swamper grinned toothlessly, 'you sure look prettied up this mornin'.'

Marlene Welch was still regarded as the most handsome woman in Blue Springs Creek, despite her thirty-year-old status as a businesswoman – or spinster – and shot a scowl at the man with the mop.

'What are you even goin' on about?' she shot back, feistily. 'I am dressed as I do just about every day.'

The swamper's skepticism was thick enough to cut with a blunt knife.

'Sure – I reckon – if you say so, Miss Marlene. . . .'

'Very well, Mr Dobbs, what is the difference about the way I am dressed today?' she asked, curious.

'Well, you got your Sunday-go-to-meetin' dress on for one thing,' Andy Dobbs noted.

'What? This old thing?' she said with a smile.

'Cost you at least ten dollars at Ma Haffner's,' Dobbs observed.

Marlene Welch's eyes narrowed.

'How far would ten dollars take you, you old swamper?'

'How's that, Miss Marlene?' Dobbs replied.

'Are you too dumb to know when you are told to get busy or catch a stage?' she said without a smile.

The swamper hurried on to the front porch and got busy with mop and pail.

To alleviate the tedium a little, Marlene Welch

14

attended to most of the paperwork at her private table by the bar-room windows. As a rule, she liked to get this part of her chores out of the way early in the day. As the only woman saloon owner in the country, she could then concentrate on what she did best: greeting customers, serving drinks and keeping an eye on her staff.

She had started as a dance-hall girl back in Dodge City. It was her job to brighten the evenings of the many lonely men fresh off the trails. She was on the 'respectable' side of Front Street back then, where most establishments barred girls and gambling; but she was there for those cowboys starved of female companionship. As a saloon girl she would sing for the men, dance with them and talk to them, inducing them to remain in the bar, buying drink after drink and patronizing the gaming tables.

Like most saloon girls she was a refugee from her family's farm in Tennessee, which had been destroyed by the Civil War. She earned as much as ten dollars a week and worked her way up to earning commission from the drinks she helped sell. Whiskey sold to the customer was generally marked up thirty to sixty per cent over the wholesale price. Commonly, drinks brought for the girls, such as Marlene, would only be cold tea or colored sugar water served in a shot glass; however, the customers were charged the full price of whiskey, which could range from ten to seventy-five cents a shot. Marlene Welch was learning the business.

Marlene doubted if she would get far with her

ledger this morning, however. The day following Dorothy Daniels' funeral would be no ordinary day. Shock waves were still reverberating around the town in the wake of the tragedy – and the dramatic return of Frank Daniels had stirred Blue Springs Creek, too. Marlene had never seen the town so disinterested in its everyday business.

Marlene Welch's main purpose in sitting at her table this particular morning was to see what was going on, and maybe to be seen.

The rain had blown away overnight, leaving mud and slush in its wake. A pallid sun had broken through the cloud cover by mid-morning. By noon, steam was rising from the street.

Looking up from her books, Marlene saw a wagon grinding by. The wheels and the team were caked with mud. Men from the hardware store were laying planks across the street for pedestrians, and the first person to cross over with dry boots was Melvin Pasley.

Atticus the horse breaker wore an added aura of importance these days, having been the man who saw the killers as they thundered away from the Daniels' spread on the day of the murder. Hidden behind a stand of brush as any self-preserving horse breaker might with wild outlaws about, Atticus had an unimpeded view of the hellions who had taken five of Dorothy Daniels' blood horses with them as they left. The same day, he identified three of the five men from the sheriff's wanted files: Henry and Rhonda Lowe and Olly Murdock. As a result of Atticus' good work, the entire West knew that Dorothy Daniels had been the victim of the Murdock Gang.

After Atticus had swaggered past, Marlene Welch returned to her work. Dark haired and full figured, she was a fine-looking woman who liked to wear brightly colored ruffled skirts that maybe in her younger days were scandalously short for the time but were now considered to be a modest length. She still liked to have her arms and shoulders bare, with her bodice cut low over her bosom – all to help business.

Marlene Welch was also unique in that, despite her occupation and past, she could still boast a good reputation.

Customers had been drifting in for half an hour now, and Marlene could not help but overhear their excited conversations. Everyone was talking about developments out at the Daniels' spread since Frank's return. The latest story was that the five brothers were getting ready to go after the Murdock Gang – even Hugh with his law practice, and Virgil with a ranch to run.

Some drinkers seemed to be of the opinion that with Frank at their head, the Daniels would run down the Murdock Gang in next to no time. Others were more cautious.

The banker, Larry Niehardt, said: 'I wouldn't be too sure of that, gentlemen. I mean, all sorts of people have been trying to get Olly Murdock and his bunch for quite some time. . . .'

Marlene nodded to herself in agreement. She considered that the Daniels would be making a huge mistake by hunting that gang, even with Frank to lead them.

Her face shadowed at the thought of Frank Daniels, her former lover. Friends said that Marlene Welch still carried a torch for Frank, and that was why she had never taken an interest in anyone else since. She was still thinking of Frank when she saw him. His size made sure that he stood out amongst the group of men walking towards the jailhouse. She had measured him once: six feet five inches tall. Big Frank. He had been much younger then. That was before Frank Daniels began his wandering, building a kind of legend as a winner at just about everything he attempted.

Now he was back, right here in Blue Springs Creek – but not for long. Marlene could tell just by his look that it would not be for much longer. Frank Daniels never forgave a wrong.

Marlene doubted that he could do it, even if he tried or wanted to.

Marlene was leaning half out of her chair to watch until the voice behind her said, 'Is that Frank Daniels?' She leaned back in her chair and looked up at Lucy Keller, the Bella Union's sweet-voiced singer and Marlene's surrogate daughter.

'Oh, you startled me, sugar,' Marlene Welch said. 'Yes, that is Frank. The big fella.'

Lucy, pale and slender, moved to the window to take her first look at the man all of Blue Springs Creek was making a fuss about. She did not enjoy good health and had missed yesterday's funeral with

18

a high temperature. Marlene mothered her, and thoroughly approved of her keeping company with Casey Daniels.

Lucy rubbed her arms as though cold.

'Is it true that they are all going, Marlene?' she asked softly.

'I am afraid so, sugar. All of those boys,' Marlene replied simply.

'Will . . . will they be all right?'

Marlene Welch looked away before she began her reply. 'Well. . . .'

'I would like the truth, Marlene. You seem to understand about things like this. One of the girls said that the Murdock Gang will kill them all if they go chasin' after them.'

Marlene stood up and put her arms around the girl's slim shoulders.

'What nonsense. I will not hear such things. They are just another bunch of hellions, nothing special about the Murdock Gang.'

'I would die if anything happened to Casey,' the girl said, already looking tearful at the awful thought.

'Nothin' will . . .' Marlene hesitated and then added, 'What say I try and get Frank to change his mind?'

Lucy grabbed her shoulder.

'Oh, would you do that for me? Would you really ask him to do that? Marlene, when will you see him?'

Marlene Welch smiled as she answered, 'He will come to see me. I guarantee it.'

Lucy studied her face.

'You are still in love with him, aren't you, Marlene?
I can see it in your eyes.'

'Will you please go and let me get on with my
work?' Marlene replied. The girl lingered before she
added, 'Go on . . . go on . . . shoo!'

It was a long time before Frank Daniels came to
the Bella Union Saloon, but he came. He and
Marlene embraced warmly, like old friends. At least
that was how it was supposed to be, but for Marlene
Welch it would always be something else. It was her
secret that Frank Daniels had spoiled her for anyone
else. If it were possible for someone to be too much
of a man, then that was Frank – too big, too strong,
too stubborn, too iron-willed, too everything. And
too much his own relentless man, so it seemed, to be
somebody's husband.

'You look well, Frank, considering what you have
been up to.'

'And you are lovelier than ever, Marlene girl.'

To her, his deep voice had always held the secret
comfort of a stream running over smooth stones. She
touched his cheek in sympathy, then moved back to
look him over.

'Are you all right, Frank?'

He nodded silently as he took out his cigar case.
Frank Daniels looked older than his thirty-nine years,
with the deep bronze of his skin and the lines in his
face. Yet his body was that of a younger man, broad
of shoulder and narrow of hip, with thick arms and
long legs. This was a man of the open spaces. Today,
as always, Marlene felt that she sensed the clean

breath of the far places coming off him, bringing the old excitement.

'Don't do this, Frank,' she heard herself say.

The blue Daniels eyes looked at her sharply. 'What? Hunt them down? Of course I will do it, Marlene. For my mother,' he paused. 'Somebody has to.'

'Not you,' she said. 'Why does it have to be you?'

Frank bit off the tip of the cigar and spat it away. He scraped a match into flame and sucked the cigar into life.

'You are goin' to start lecturing me, aren't you?'

'Frank, the Murdock Gang isn't like other gangs. Everybody says so. There are too many of them and they are too dangerous, and everyone who mixes with them gets themselves . . .'

His eyes were glacial now. '. . . killed?' He took a breath. 'They murdered my mother in cold blood. What do you expect me to do?'

She took his hands in hers. 'Frank, darling . . . it is too late to help your mother now. And even if it wasn't, you would be the wrong man to go after them . . .'

'What the hell do you mean by that, Marlene?' his voiced boomed.

She squeezed his big hands.

'You know what I mean, Frank. You hate too hard; you do everything too hard. You would go on after those outlaws or anyone else, and nothing would stop you, not even if you knew you would die. Don't you understand, Frank? It isn't worth it. You could

21

get killed. You could all be killed. All of your brothers. And what good would that do your dear mother
– Dorothy? Tell me that.'

He pulled away from her, his face closing.

'I have got things to attend to . . .'

Marlene was getting desperate.

'Frank, if you have to go, please go alone. Don't
take the boys with you.'

He moved towards the door, and now the seamed
face was expressionless.

'There would be none of them would stay behind.
They lost their mother too.'

'Well, at least not Casey,' Marlene insisted. 'Not
the kid.'

But Frank just shook his head and went through
the batwing doors, his shoulders seeming to fill the
doorway. Watching him cross the street on the
planks, Marlene stood with her hands clasped tightly
to her middle as though in pain. . . .

'Don't go . . . don't go, my love,' she whispered.
She knew all the while that he would. Whoever did
Frank Daniels wrong and got away with it?

Marlene Welch went to the bar and ordered a
double. She would need it before telling Lucy the
bad news.

Glancing out at the street again, she glimpsed
Frank standing on the porch of the law office with his
four brothers. They were looking at him as though
he were some kind of god.

CHAPTER 2

HARD NEWS AND HARD CASES

The Indian pony twitched its ears and turned its small head to stare into the black patches of moon shadow where four white men went very still, staring back at the horse with unblinking eyes. After a time, the pony went back to grazing on its tether rope. Henry Lowe was able to reach out slowly to mash the midge that had sunk its proboscis deep into his neck.

Henry signaled, and his comrades inched forward – cousin Newson Murdock and two more distant kinsmen. They were after the Indians' horses. The gang had been short of horses ever since leaving the Indian Nations, and even the raid on the ranch in Missouri had only secured them a handful of mounts. Henry, with a major job planned for which extra horses were needed, was getting desperate. You had to be desperate to try and steal horses off wild Indians.

Like figures from a badman's nightmare, the feathered riders loomed black against the night sky, exploding into a headlong charge as they came down the steep slope, howling and screaming and waving murderous lances that flashed in the moonlight.

The Indians came straight at them, proving that they were far from surprised. Dark-faced and muscular and bent on killing, they came charging across the grass past the tethered ponies, sounding more like wolves than men as they closed in. Before they reached their quarry, the outlaw guns overrode their cries. Three of their number went down in threshing heaps.

A horse with a broken leg lunged into another rider, causing his mount to lose its footing. The buck threw himself into the air and landed with cat-like agility on the balls of his feet. He emitted a blood-curdling shriek, rattled his feathered tomahawk, and took one mighty leap forward, only to run headlong into a slug from Henry Lowe's pistol.

Lowe grunted in satisfaction as he rolled behind a deadfall. But one of his men went down under a storm of unshod hoofs. Lowe heard him howl in pain. It was a sound he wouldn't be able to remove from his mind any time soon.

Touching off another two shots, Lowe dropped flat to reload while his two remaining men kept the enemy at bay. The Indians whirled away and circled, coming straight back at them in a charge as they filled the air with arrows.

'Lucky they don't have rifles,' Ernie Gross shouted, ducking low as a whistling arrow parted his hair. He quickly felt to see if it had cut him, and it had just barely.

It was Henry Lowe's turn to duck as a spinning tomahawk hissed close to his face. Bobbing up, he pumped three screaming slugs into a rushing figure. He rolled aside and kept rolling as the dead horse and rider smashed into the space where he had just been.

The fierce fight ebbed and flowed for several minutes as the outlaws fought their way back to a nest of rocks on a low hill. A spear came within an inch of pinning Lowe to the dirt. Moments later, a reckless buck put his mount into a spectacular leap that carried him right over their heads. The rider swung an ax that split a wounded outlaw's skull as though it were a ripe melon.

These goddamn crazed Indians meant business!

Henry was turning away from the spurting blood as a lithe figure dived over the rocks and fell on him, one hand clawing for his throat and the other wielding a knife. Unable to use his Colts at such close range, Henry Lowe butted and smashed the buck's nose and blood ran down into the buck's mouth. Next he elbowed the buck in the Adam's apple. The Indian was choking from blood in his mouth and lack of air and going black in the face as he fell away. At that very moment, a bowstring snapped, and Lowe heard the hiss of an arrow. He ducked, hoping he wasn't too late. The shaft slammed into the choking Indian, the arrow piercing his eye – it drove him screaming from the rocks.

Lowe's brutal laughter sounded as the Indian buck let out a yip of emotion, seeing his bloody mistake. He had made a second one. The white man now had room to use his pistols and use them he did.

But there was no time to gloat for Henry Lowe. Another of his men was gone, and now it was just two of them, himself and Newson Murdock, against a superior number of enemies. How many Indians, Lowe wasn't sure, but the answer was simple – too damn many. This would have been plain to a blind man, Henry's father used to say – but if Lowe saw it, he showed no sign.

'Back to back!' he ordered in a roar, the whites of his eyes showing in the smoky moonlight. They pressed their broad backs together, and Newson Murdock grinned over a broad shoulder as each man reloaded and waited for the next onslaught to start.

'The poor bastards, Lowe. They still think they can lick us!'

This wasn't bravado: it was the spirit that made the Murdock Gang something special. There was no doubt that Murdock and the gang were murderous human vermin who deserved to dance at the end of a rope. That description fitted several hundred men in the sparsely populated West. The Murdock bunch stood out in the crowd because they believed that they were unbeatable. A lot of folks on both sides of the law had come to that assessment of the gang.

The spirit of the gang came from Henry Lowe, a man who it seemed was born for battle.

With two men slaughtered and another wave of blood-hungry riders coming at them in a rush, the outlaws stood back to back with their chests and guns out and chins high.

Riding with the fury of thieves who had suffered a theft, the leading savage bore down on the rock nest relentlessly, his wicked lance tucked beneath his right arm. The heavy spearhead was held steady and pointed straight at Henry Lowe's heart.

At the last possible moment, Lowe's pistol roared, and the bullet swatted the Indian from the bony back of his pony.

The others kept coming in a dark flood. The bad man had just a handful of seconds to wonder if, after all, this might be the fight they would not win.

Murdock's heavy revolvers churned as two racing figures sped close. The recoil of the guns pulsed through his big body into Lowe's back. Then Lowe's weapons chimed in. The sensation of shared violence was like a drug, keeping them fighting, killing, and somehow staving off the end – that is, until the enemy was 'wedged.'

The wedge that split their ranks was a tight bunch of horsemen who came around the shoulder of the low hill. Roaring gunfire cut into the Indians' ranks. Outlaw horses used weight and momentum to knock the Indian mustangs off their feet.

Riding at the head of the relief was an old man

with silver hair flowing behind him and a sawn-off shotgun clasped in his heavy hands.

Uncle Birch Murdock, Newson Murdock's older brother.

Behind him came other members of the gang and hangers-on, all rebel yelling, all shooting like there was no tomorrow.

'The old bastard!' Henry Lowe breathed aloud and Newson turned to take a look, powerful teeth showing in a huge grin.

'I should've knowed . . . he said all along that we were crazy to hit this camp . . .' Newson added.

Then an arrow thrummed close – too close. With a roar of pure relish, Lowe sprang forward to seize a powerful buck by the topknot. The outlaw jammed the muzzle of his pistol against the Indian's ear and jerked the trigger.

He flung the corpse aside and went after another quarry. Newson joined him. Body piled upon body and blood ran like rain water as the short, fierce skirmish reached its raging climax and then ebbed into hard-breathing silence.

The outlaws would happily have gone on killing, but there were no Indians left to kill. A boy too young to have earned a feather for his hair was still groaning weakly. That feeble show of life drew enough lead to wipe out ten men.

Henry Lowe leapt nimbly backwards as a wounded horse fell against him.

'Told you,' Olly Murdock growled behind his brother and gang member.

'So you did, you old bastard,' Newson Murdock grinned.

'How many men did you lose?' the older Murdock brother inquired.

Both Newson's and Henry's grins faded fast.

'We don't lose men, dammit! Some just don't make it back, is all,' Henry answered.

The bad old man nodded like a pupil absorbing a valuable fact. None admired Olly Murdock like the members of his gang, especially his younger brother. Olly Murdock had always aspired to become an outlaw hero, but his own career in the dark brotherhood had been totally unremarkable, until his younger brother Newson and his best friend, Henry Lowe, grew to manhood and showed him how it should be done.

Henry was a natural. Even his worst enemies said that. His father always suspected his boy would turn bad. Nonetheless, Olly and the rest were proud to be in his presence, despite the gang being named for Olly.

The outlaws rounded up the Indian ponies and rode back to their camp at an easy pace. They left their dead for the scavengers. There were no burial rites in the Murdock Gang, and mourning was a sign of weakness.

Leading a string of three paint ponies, Newson Murdock called to the 'unofficial' leader of the gang, Henry Lowe.

'Have we got enough horses, now, Henry?'

'Enough for what?' Lowe called back.

'For whatever it is you have in store for us next,' Newson replied.

'Who says I have something in store for the gang?'

Henry Lowe was not fooling anybody. Ever since the gang had suffered one of its few reverses and had been driven out of the Indian Nations by a federal posse, Lowe had been after replacement horses. Down at Blue Springs Creek they had even taken the risk of hitting a big horse ranch, only to find that the main herd was elsewhere, on the summer range. Their raid on the Indians had produced a score of hardy Indian ponies – nothing like the quality of the five horses from the Daniels spread, but these horses had stamina, even so.

A rough count now indicated that there were at least two mounts for each member of the twenty-man gang.

Even when Newson's father pressed to know what Henry Lowe was planning, the outlaw leader only said, 'If I want to advertise, I can always run a few lines in the papers.' And no one questioned him again. When it was time for the rest of the gang to know, he would tell them.

CHAPTER 3

TRAIL OF BLOOD

'Hurry up and wait,' Virgil Daniels said wryly. 'It's just like being in the army again.'

'There he goes, braggin' about his fightin' days again,' smiled Hugh.

'Nothin' worse than when old guys get to reminiscin' about days past, is there?' added Casey. 'Like old ranchers and attorneys, I mean. Ain't that so, Urban?'

Urban Daniels was not making the same effort to keep the mood light that his brothers were. In truth, he disapproved of banter at a time like this. His tanned face was sober as he continued to stare out of the ranch-house window at the man they were all watching: Frank.

'He is sure takin' his time,' was Urban's comment.

'That is what I said,' rancher Virgil reminded him. 'Hurry up and wait. He didn't give us five minutes to decide that we all wanted to ride with him, but now he acts like we have nothin' to do and all day to do it in.'

'I guess Frank knows what he's doin',' Hugh said seriously, leaning on the sill.

'He always did,' affirmed Virgil, using that tone bordering on awe that was often noticeable in the Daniels brothers when they spoke of their eldest brother. He nodded. 'He's readin' signs now. Trackin' was just another thing he always did better than just about anybody I ever seen or knew.'

'I guess Frank was just blessed,' Hugh said thoughtfully. 'As far back as I can remember, it seems he could always do anything he put his mind to.'

Nobody debated that. All of the four tall men gathered in the front room of their parents' ranch house at the moment had grown up in the shadow of their big brother. It had never occurred to any of them to resent the fact that almost nothing they ever did seemed to measure up to Frank's achievements. Riding, shooting, swimming, dancing, fighting or even winning women, Frank set a standard that only a fool would try to surpass.

A major factor in this absence of jealousy had always been Frank's own personality and manner. The giant of a man never bragged or rubbed it in. He just went ahead and did things that other men only dreamed about.

'Hey, he is finally movin' our way,' Virgil remarked. 'Could be he has seen enough.'

There was impatience in Virgil's makeup. He

wanted to be out there on the tracks of those outlaws right now. He wanted them all dead or in jail and himself back with his wife on his own spread.

He wanted to start overcoming the pain. In this he appeared very different from Frank, who seemed to have simply accepted the pain. It was always hard to say just what Frank thought and felt. There had always been something mysterious about him, even when the boys were growing up, and that quality seemed to have strengthened as he grew older. He hadn't even told them where he had been or what he'd been doing when he belatedly heard about their mother's death.

On the other end of all this scrutiny, Frank paused in the yard to glance back at the area he had been scouring for the past hour. The outlaw tracks were a week old now, and largely obscured by others, but he knew them all. Five men had come to their mother's ranch, and now he would recognize the prints of those five horses anyplace.

He took out his cigar case. It was silver, well worn. Everything that Frank Daniels owned or wore was good. Not flash, just solid quality. And most of what he owned was the equipment of the nomad – horse, bedroll, weapons, boots and clothing. His shirts were tailored for his broad shoulders, and his dark pants were cut to fit comfortably over the tops of bench-made boots of fine black leather. His guns, snugged in plain holsters, had thornwood grips and a gull finish. The foresights of both six-shooters were filed away, for sights could snag on leather when a man went to draw.

Frank's roving gaze rested on the cottonwood by the family barn. As a kid, he used to climb that tree and jump for his father to catch him – and Isaac never missed. Isaac Daniels had been a big man then, in his natural prime. Booming and self-assured. He grew quieter as he got older, leaving it to his strapping sons to make most of the noise and handle most of the work.

A good man. Simple and straight. The same could be said of the boys' mother. His father had been gone a few years, and now the woman who had shared his life for nearly forty years. But she had died not from illness, accident, act of God or sheer misfortune, but at the hand of men – and one man in particular. A man who was still breathing. . . .

Frank turned to face the window where four faces, each one similar to his own in at least one major respect, stared out at him.

'I'm ready boys,' he called, his voice loud. 'Let's saddle up!'

The last man the brothers spoke to before leaving Blue Springs Creek an hour or so later was Melvin Pasley, the wrangler, the horse breaker, the only citizen actually to see the killers.

Considering the challenge of what they were undertaking, the Daniels brothers had to be sure beyond all doubt who they were after. Melvin had already furnished detailed descriptions of the outlaws, but Frank wanted him to go through it with him all over again.

Since the tragedy, the brothers had made it their business to familiarize themselves with everything the law office was able to supply on the men who comprised the Murdock Gang. It didn't take the brothers long, listening to Melvin, to know there could be no possible mistake. Melvin described Henry and Rhonda Lowe, Atticus Gartels, 'Gila' Murdock, and Newson and Uncle Birch Murdock.

Five murderous members of the Murdock Gang.

In Frank's hand were five black stones from a flowerpot in the little courtyard at his mother's ranch where she and his father had sat every fine evening for nearly forty years. They had found the stones clasped in her dead hand. It had been the dying woman's way of telling her boys the number of her killers.

The stones were Frank Daniels' now.

Blue Springs Creek had not seen an occasion like it since the war, when young men went off to fight with the Missouri Volunteers. Virtually the whole town was out to see them off, and a serious, emotional occasion it was. Grim-faced men and tearful women looked proud and relieved and angry all at once. Nobody could undo what had been done, their attitude said, but at least now something was being done.

There was no doubt that the town's mood would have been completely different if Frank had not turned up to lead the vengeance posse. Nobody would suggest that Hugh, Virgil, Casey and Urban were anything but strong and purposeful men, but to tackle the Murdock Gang was a daunting task by any standard. The only reason that Blue Springs Creek felt hopeful was the man riding the barrel-chested dark brown thoroughbred up front.

All the well-documented Frank Daniels stories had seen wide circulation since his dramatic return. Young folks and newcomers had heard about his epic, twenty-round victory over the British heavyweight bare-knuckle champion at just eighteen years of age; his survival alone on Mount Ellen Peak for nearly six weeks when cut off by snow; the recurring rumors that he owned a gold mine in Utah and a cattle ranch in Texas but preferred to drift and look for excitement.

The general conclusion was that the infamous Murdock Gang had finally messed with the wrong man.

'Frank will nail 'em, sure enough,' the town sage had told the crowd in the saloon. 'I never saw him start in on anything he didn't finish. Those outlaws are doomed.'

'Seems I've heard that said before about that murderous bunch,' a visiting cynic had replied, 'but if memory serves me right, that gang's been ridin' free and doin' what it damn well pleases for nigh on five years. If the law and the army can't bring 'em to book, how are five men goin' to do it . . . even if one of 'em sounds like the heavyweight champeen of everything?'

The cynic was a little soured by all this talk of Frank Daniels, but the towners had faith. They would have the last laugh on the doubtful Thomases.

The Daniels traveled slowly past the Blue Springs Creek Feed and Grain, the general store, and on toward the Bella Union. Two women were on the porch at the saloon, watching what almost looked like a Fourth of July parade. But there was no joy in the occasion for Marlene Welch and Lucy Keller. Eighteen-year-old Lucy was sniffling and red-nosed because Casey was going off, maybe to get himself killed, and she believed she was in love with him. How Marlene felt about Frank nobody really knew, but she had made no secret of the fact that she considered this Daniels family vengeance crusade a grave and foolish mistake.

And she blamed it all on Frank.

'Oh, will you just look at Casey?' Lucy whimpered. 'You would think he was goin' off on a huntin' trip to have the best time of his life with his brothers.'

Casey was waving his hat to a group of friends who, like himself, were only a few years out of school. His friends cheered him, and one shouted, 'Nail one of 'em for me, Case!'

'An eye for an eye,' Marlene murmured. 'That is a line of reasonin' I have never been able to follow. Somebody knocks your eye out, so you do the same to them. Then you are both supposed to feel better. I don't think so.'

Lucy was staring at Frank now, taking in his width of shoulder, the bronzed ruggedness of his features, the way he sat his saddle with a hand resting on his thigh and his elbow crooked away from his body, a picture of rugged power without any hint of vanity.

'Is he as fine as they say, Miss Marlene?' the girl asked. If her Casey had to go, God alone knew where, to hunt a gang of killers, it would help Lucy to know that he was being looked after. Marlene's eyes were on Frank's face. He was staring straight ahead as they approached the saloon, but she knew he would look up. He would have to.

Marlene Welch did not see him as 'the heavy-weight champeen of everything'. She saw a man that she knew and loved. She saw a man who could kill or be killed, the same as any other man.

'They should not be going,' she said, knowing that was not the response Lucy wanted or needed to hear.

'Will he look out for Casey?' the young woman pressed her. 'Will he care for him? He's only a boy, for Pete's sake.'

'Oh, Frank will look out for them all. Have no fear about that. But what good will it do? They are four ordinary men going after a small army of professional killers. No amount of care or looking after can guarantee their safety.'

Lucy Keller frowned.

'You said four, Miss Marlene. There are five of 'em.'

'I don't put Frank in with his brothers. That would be like countin' a wolf in with the house dogs.'

The riders had halted because a weaving drunk had staggered into the street to exhort them to victory. Lucy turned to face her employer squarely, her mouth tight at the corners.

'Miss Marlene, I just don't understand you some days. I honestly can't figure if you love that man, Frank Daniels, or hate his guts.'

'What does it matter?' Marlene said coldly. 'I am probably seein' him for the last time anyway.'

'But Miss Marlene, they say that Frank Daniels just does not know how to lose at anything,' the young Lucy replied.

Marlene turned her head away and said, 'Everybody loses sooner or later. Everybody.'

Lucy gave up and moved away a little. She was down enough without hearing talk like that. Marlene's face was blank, but she was feeling things – of that, Lucy was sure. She was feeling things like somebody was sticking knives into her.

The sheriff ushered the drunk on to the board-walk, and the horsemen came on. Hugh Daniels looked a little out of character, wearing an attorney's jacket and a Colt .45. Rancher Virgil smoked his pipe and waved back to his wife, who had come to see them off. It was plain to everyone that Casey wanted to ride up to the saloon and say goodbye to his girl, but he settled for a salute and a smile. Urban the drifter stared past Frank at the hills, as though already plotting their course. Frank looked straight ahead.

But Marlene knew this man better than anyone, and as he drew level with the saloon, he turned his head sharply and stared directly at her. That did not surprise her, but then he lifted his hand to halt his brothers and turned the brown thoroughbred towards the porch.

Marlene Welch was thrilled, but she did not let it show.

'Don't ask me to wish you luck, Frank. I cannot do it.'

'I have never relied on luck, Marlene,' Frank simply replied.

Marlene looked at him. 'On what then? How tough you are?'

His lopsided smile took her by surprise.

'Tough? I never was half as tough as you, Marlene, and don't let anyone ever tell you otherwise.'

'You're goin' to enjoy this, aren't you, Frank?'

The smile faded.

'You know I have to do this.'

'Like you did with the bear?' she fired back.

Frank stared. Then he nodded, touched his hat brim and turned his horse back into the street. Blue Springs Creek watched the Daniels boys out of sight.

Marlene Welch was working on a solitary double rye half an hour later when she looked into the bar mirror and saw Lucy standing behind her. The girl was smiling.

'I have decided to be brave, Miss Marlene. I am not goin' to spend the whole of the next week or month getting around with red eyes and a runny nose. I am going to be cheerful and happy and patient until they all come back.'

A sarcastic reply came to Marlene Welch's lips, but

it died there. She even managed a smile as she turned on her high stool.

'I'm glad to hear it, sweetie,' she said. 'And who knows? Maybe I have been a bit gloomy about it all myself. Maybe I should try and be happy, too.'

'You do love him, don't you, Miss Marlene? I saw it in your face when you two were talkin'.'

'What is love?' Marlene shrugged.

'What did you mean by what you said?'

Marlene Welch eyed the girl strangely. 'About what?'

'The bear. I didn't understand that,' Lucy explained.

'It's not important.'

'It seemed to be. Please, tell me, Miss Marlene.'

Marlene sighed. She was tired. Maybe she was getting old.

'You mean to say you don't know the story about Frank Daniels and the bear?'

'No.'

'A grizzly came down out of the mountains and took Frank's favorite horse. So, naturally he went after it. But this was a travelin' bear, and Frank was still huntin' it two months later in the mountains. Caught it, too. Only thing, he wounded the bear with his rifle and it attacked him and almost tore his arm off before he could kill it.'

Marlene stopped, and Lucy said, 'Well, there must be more to it than that.'

'There is. The arm got poisoned, and a doctor in the north wanted to cut it off. But Frank said no. He

41

came back home by train and was laid up for six months. Just think of that, Lucy. Six months of agony and operations just because he went after a dumb old bear.'

'But men do dumb things like that all the time, Miss Marlene. It is their way.'

'Not the way Frank Daniels does them. Other men hunt because they want to. Frank does it because it he has to. That is the terrible difference. A man doin' somethin' because he wants to can stop anytime, but a man who has to, is different. He keeps on, even if he knows he might lose an arm . . . or his life.'

'I think you are makin' too much of it, Miss Marlene, if you don't mind me sayin' so,' Lucy added.

'Sweetie, you still don't understand. Even after he had lost six months of his life over a bear, Frank still thought he had won something.'

CHAPTER 4

A BIG MAN RIDING

Where the rivers flowed together, the terrain was flat and in places marshy and overgrown with rushes. The combined waters formed a lake with a scattering of low islands. Back from the banks and the small patches of sandy beaches, the ground sloped upwards into brush-covered hummocks. It was on one of these islands that the Daniels found remnants of a recent camp, and it didn't take long for Frank to be certain that the Murdock Gang had been there.

His brothers were pleased, for sign-reading throughout that day had been difficult and uncertain. The weather, in the form of wind or rain, could degrade signs. It was not sufficient to just look at a foot or hoofprint from one point of view. At certain times Frank knew that the sun and shadow could distort a print, and that a tracker, such as he was, might have to study them from multiple angles.

Frank Daniels felt he needed to get close to the tracks without disturbing them, and an up-close look could provide small details he might otherwise overlook.

The brothers could not understand why Frank did not share their happy reaction.

He explained over a hearty supper of fresh venison and sourdough.

'These outlaws don't do anything without a reason,' Frank said, 'and I think I know the reason they came out here.'

Casey glanced at Urban. As a drifter and a man of the outdoors, Urban was regarded as a sign reader and tracker not far below Frank's standards. Casey's look was asking Urban what he thought, and Urban was quick with his answer.

'You figure they are goin' to take to the water for a while, Frank?' he asked.

'On target.' Frank was chewing roasted meat. He was a neat eater, wiping his fingers fastidiously on a bandanna after every mouthful. He had shaved before supper and was the only one with the energy to do so.

'If I was tryin' to shake off pursuit, I would head straight for this kind of country myself.' He swallowed and added, 'We could have our work cut out for us in the mornin' boys, tryin' to find where they left the lake.'

A fish plopped in the water, and the moon was a shimmer of silver on the horizon. The meal over, Casey cleaned the plates by rubbing them with sand.

Urban and Virgil tended the horses. Hugh strolled across to the hummock where Frank stood with a cigar, waiting for the moon.

'We've done well so far, wouldn't you say, Frank?'

Hugh had a measured way of speaking. Like any good attorney, he considered his words before speaking. Seven years younger than Frank, he was almost as tall but not nearly as broad – few were. Although he had exchanged his towner's coat for a hip-length leather jacket, Hugh still looked awkward with a pistol buckled to his hip.

'We can do even better,' was Frank's response.

Hugh was silent as he fashioned a cigarette. He did so one-handed, a trick he had picked up from his father and never forgotten.

'I'm missin' Jane already.' He licked the cigarette into a cylinder. 'Just thought I should let you know.'

'Your wife's a fine woman. Why wouldn't you miss her?'

'Yes . . . yes, she is that . . .' With his smoke going to his satisfaction, Hugh watched the moon make its timid appearance over the marshlands and lake. He cleared his throat. 'Of course, she doesn't approve of what we are doing. . . .'

Frank's smile was humorless.

'She could join the rest of the women and make a club.'

Hugh lifted his eyebrows. 'Marlene Welch?'

'Marlene.' Frank exhaled a gust of blue smoke and filled his chest with air. 'Of course, all women are the same, Hugh. If someone does them wrong, their response is to weep and carry on, whereas a man will do somethin' about it.'

'Guess you're right.' Hugh was thoughtfully silent for a time. 'Though I guess it is fair to say we are takin' on about the worst there is, isn't that so?'

'They have got a bad reputation.'

'I hear about them in my work. Part of this reputation they have is that nobody's ever even looked like getting the better of them. That indicates we are setting ourselves a tall order, now, doesn't it?'

'That is the truth,' Frank said with a slight sigh. 'Tall enough.'

Frank held out his clenched fist, turned it face up, uncurled his fingers. Five black stones glittered in the light of the new moon.

'And we are goin' to fill it,' he said quietly.

Hugh wanted to say more about the Murdock Gang, but it did not seem like the right time. While waiting for sleep later, he found himself wondering if he was less of a man because he did not seem to hate as hard as his older brother, Frank.

As Frank predicted, the next day was rough. Real rough. It was spent combing the wetlands for a sign that they did not find. They camped on the same island that night, and first light found them leaving the lake behind and heading for the nearest town, Frank and Urban agreeing that they could not afford to waste any more time and must look for leads elsewhere.

Arnold Groves was a one-horse town where they served fine beefsteak at a sprawling eatery named

The Greasy Spoon. Part Indian and a yard wide, the proprietor, Bart McNulty, proved an unexpected source of information.

'The Murdock Gang you are after, big feller?' he said to Frank. 'Hell, of course I know somethin' about 'em. They carved up half of my kin four nights back out at Caprock Ridge, didn't they?'

'They did?' Frank said. 'Are you certain?'

Bart McNulty was sure enough. The Indians had brought two dead white men to Arnold Groves, and papers they were carrying identified them as fugitives and members of the Murdock Gang. The outlaws had stolen a dozen ponies and were last seen heading for the lakes region.

That put the Daniels back where they started, but before nightfall, their relentless interrogation of the locals bore fruit. Urban encountered a wheezy old hide hunter, in town for a bender. The man revealed that he had heard a large number of riders go past his place on Sycamore Creek three nights earlier, give or take a few hours.

It was anything but a definite lead, but it was something. And it paid off.

Next day at first light, Frank Daniels was squatting on a grassy brown hill a mile or so from Sycamore Creek.

The earth all around him was churned by hoof tracks, several days old, but clear enough still for Frank to make out. The prints were from a mixture of shod horses and Indian ponies.

Frank made positive identification of some of the

shod horses that had come from his mother's place.

Having left Arnold Groves long before breakfast, the brothers stopped to fix food and coffee before taking off along the tracks which snaked northwest, towards the hill country and woods.

'Huntin' and trappin' country,' Urban announced as they put the miles behind them. 'Out of the way, and no towns. Why would bad outlaws want to come right out here?'

'Maybe they are just plain yellow scared of us?' Casey joked, thumping his chest. 'Maybe all they are thinkin' about is losin' us.'

'No sign that they know we are after them yet, kid,' Frank said.

'How do you figure that?' Casey wanted to know.

'They would likely do something about it if they knew,' Frank explained to his younger brother.

'Well, they tried to shake us off at the marshes,' the youngest Daniels' brother noted.

'That might have been to lose any Indians doggin' them after the horse raid,' Frank went on to clarify.

'They sure seem hungry for horses, this outfit,' said Virgil with a grimace. 'Seems they don't care how many people they kill to get what they want, either.'

His words cast a silence over the brothers. For a long time, each man was back at the family ranch, picturing their father trying to defend what was his.

Their pace picked up instinctively. The faster they rode, the sooner the day of reckoning.

CHAPTER 5

CURTAINS FOR
FRANK DANIELS

Stealing the furs was the easy part: it would be keeping them that might prove testing. Henry Lowe knew all that long before he visited Boojum's Camp deep in the wilderness. He had taken precautions, mainly in providing a remount for each of his butchers for the long run out.

Security was low at the camp where bearded Boojum and nine brawling trappers had been working for months assembling a high value stash of beaver and silver fox. The last thieves who had tried to get at those furs had been run down by the hard-riding trappers in the first hour and hanged in the second.

'Who needs locks?' Boojum was fond of saying. 'The plains are the walls of my safe.'

There were howls and curses and warning shots fired in the air after the theft was discovered. Within minutes, the trappers were mounted and following the tracks of the wagon which the thieves had used to transport the pelts.

'To steal a man's furs and his wagon to carry 'em?' Boojum thundered, red-faced and outraged. 'Hangin' will be too good for 'em.'

There was no doubt in his mind that he would run the thieves down, but when he hadn't caught up with them by dawn, he began to have misgivings. When there was still no sign of them by noon, Boojum realized that the thieves were using remounts, and were smarter than anyone who had tried to rob him before.

Marshal John Blythe was a big, heavy-framed man of fifty with a tangled mane of shaggy hair which lay back from his sloping forehead and overflowed his collar at the back. His nose was thin and hooked sharply like an eagle's. His mouth was a deep-lined canyon between the peak of his nose and the stubborn bulge of his jaw.

Although Marshal Blythe looked less like a lawman and more like a man from the mountains, the law was his profession and he was good at it. His reputation as a manhunter was impressive, although less so than it had been a year ago, when he was given the special task of putting paid to Murdock's Gang.

'This band of butchers is a scourge of the entire West and an affront and an insult to law enforcement throughout the nation,' the chief marshal had claimed on the day they had given Blythe his roving brief. 'And until they are brought to book, the law of the West will not be able rightly to claim to be in control.'

That was a year ago now, but the words still applied. Murdock's Gang still thrived, and Marshal John Blythe looked about ten years older.

During the winter, Henry Lowe had mockingly printed a 'Wanted' dodger on the marshal, offering ten cents reward. Marshal Blythe carried a copy of that dodger in his billfold and looked at it sometimes when he was feeling exceptionally low. He felt that way now, but did not produce the dodger. Too many people about – people such as his deputy marshals and the sheriff of Blue Springs Creek, who was furnishing details of yet another crime attributed to the outlaws he had failed to catch.

Marshal Blythe sat by the jail-house door, whittling a piece of willow. He looked a dull man, but was in truth clever, intuitive and tenacious. Those qualities had not so far been enough to put paid to Henry Lowe – the Murdock Gang – and his clan of brothers, cousins and hangers-on, and sometimes the terrible thought invaded Marshal John Blythe's mind that Henry Lowe was just too damned smart for him or anybody else to catch.

The marshal sat up and paid more attention on learning that the Daniels brothers had gone after the outlaw gang.

This was bad news: it could mean more killings

were in store.

'Oh, this is wonderful,' he said ironically. 'This is the kind of thing the Murdock Gang expects and waits for. They love amateurs. Henry Lowe will eat them for breakfast.' Blythe snorted disgustedly. 'You can say goodbye to your local heroes, Sheriff. You'll be lucky if you see any of them alive again.'

The deputy marshals nodded in unanimous agreement. They had calluses on their hands from digging graves for victims of the Murdock Gang. But the sheriff of Blue Springs Creek did not agree.

'I can tell you I would not like to have Frank Daniels on my trail, Marshal, even if my name was Billy the Kid, Jesse James or Henry Lowe.'

'Me neither,' the deputy agreed. 'Big Frank once tracked down a grizzly bear years ago, and kilt the big bastard with his Bowie knife, so he did.'

The marshal sighed. Spare him from small town heroes! They were more trouble than they were worth.

'I guess we had best be ridin', men,' Marshal John Blythe said, getting up ponderously.

The deputies looked dismayed. They had been four days in the saddle to reach Blue Springs Creek and were walking on their heels. The marshal had promised them rest here, in real beds under a real roof.

'Sorry,' Blythe said, 'but it is not just a matter of takin' off after the gang now. We gotta try and save this here bunch of Daniels afore the Murdock Gang and Henry Lowe carve 'em up like so many

Thanksgivin' turkeys.'

'It is as plain as the nose on my face that you have never met Frank Daniels,' the sheriff said sharply. 'Otherwise you wouldn't talk that way about him and his brothers.'

'He might be every bit the man you say he is, Sheriff,' Blythe sighed. 'I wouldn't know. But I know the Murdock Gang and especially Henry Lowe, and it is just possible nobody can nail him, and that sure as hell must go for a bunch of small towners all steamed up over their mother getting' done in.'

Marshal John Blythe was not aware of it, but he was starting to talk like a beaten man. That did not mean he would give up – no, not by any stretch. He did not know how to give up. And it was a strange thing that three men sharing that uncommon characteristic were involved in the very same manhunt now – the marshal, Henry Lowe himself, and Frank Daniels. It stood to reason that sooner or later, somebody would have to quit, either voluntarily or through the gates of Boothill.

The smart money said it would not be Henry Lowe.

From the heights, the landscape ahead looked like a relief map with the earth a cloudy green and brown haze under the vast vault of the sky, reaching into the infinity that no man could ever reach. Looking down, Frank Daniels saw the river gleaming like molten lead, curving slowly and gracefully across the buffalo plains towards the mountains. The sun, the hills, the plains and the sky never really changed, he was thinking. Only man changed, yet in so many ways remained the same.

Riders were reining up on the river bank now, pointing up at Frank and gesturing. Frank watched them for some time before turning the dark brown thoroughbred back to the draw where he picked up his brothers and headed down by the animal trail.

'Could be trouble,' he warned. 'Looks like a bunch of trappers yonder. They seem mighty excited about something.'

'How will we handle it, Frank?' asked Virgil.

Frank palmed his pistol so fast that Casey gasped loud enough for all to hear.

He said, 'Nobody is goin' to stop us and we are not goin' to be slowed down, either. As far as we can see, the outlaws got one hell of a head start. That does not suit me. If we don't make up time, they are goin' to give us the slip. It's as simple as that.'

Riding behind him, his brothers exchanged a look. Throughout their week in his company, the Daniels had come to depend on Frank and to admire him more than ever. On the trail, he was the surest, strongest leader it was possible to find. There was the odd occasion, like now, however, when he seemed just a little too ruthless for their taste. The brothers did not want to get into a fight with a bunch of trappers over nothing.

As they cleared the timberline, they could see the trappers. The Daniels were crossing a series of shallow craters. The vitreous smoothness of the stone threw back the sunlight, causing the horsemen to squint as they watched the trappers.

Several of the trappers toted rifles, and when one angled his weapon towards the brothers, Frank hefted his .45 and called a warning.

'Use that thing or put it down. If you elect to use it, you are all dead.'

This was confidence. There were nine trappers. Frank acted like a man with the odds all his way, and this had its effect on the nine trappers.

Following a brief confab with the others, the rifle-man lowered his weapon. The trappers did not look any friendlier, though, as the Daniels came nearer. Truth to tell, they looked mean and dangerous men, so much so that Frank kept his revolver trained on them every step of the way. Frank's brothers were jittery. Gunplay was not the familiar thing to them that it was to him.

'Who the hell are you?' challenged a barrel-bellied man with a greasy beard. His eyes drilled into Frank as he added, 'Are you them dirty outlaws what stole our pelts?'

Instantly, Frank spun his Colt on his forefinger and dropped it back into its holster.

'No, we aren't,' Frank said, 'but we are huntin' a pack of outlaws, mister. Could be the same ones.' He tapped his chest. 'Daniels. We are all Daniels. Who are you?'

Boojum introduced himself. He was willing to take them at their word because they did not look like outlaws and there was no sign of any furs. Besides, these five men had come straight off the heights to face him, something that not even the most addle-brained thief would do.

The Daniels listened in silence to the story of the stolen furs. The trappers had pursued the thieves across the plains until their horses gave out. The thieves had remounts, Boojum informed them, though this was something the Daniels already knew.

'The Murdock Gang led by Henry Lowe now,' Frank murmured when the fat man stopped for a breath.

Boojum's eyes bulged. 'The Murdock Gang? Henry Lowe? Are you sure?'

'No question about it,' Frank replied calmly. 'Which way did they go with your furs?'

Boojum flung a hairy hand northward as he said, 'Yonder. There's a tradin' post about sixty miles that far, only by the time we got back, we wouldn't have a camp, or a trap left on account of the Utes.' He shook his shaggy head. 'Murdock's Gang! Imagine! Could be just as well we didn't catch 'em after all, huh?'

'Just as well,' Frank responded, deliberately mis-understanding. 'They belong to us.'

'Oh yeah?' another trapper said. 'Why, what did they do to you?'

Casey started to explain, but he wasn't given the time.

'Let's go,' Frank snapped, and heeled the big thoroughbred into a lope, leaving it to his brothers to make their hasty farewells as they followed.

Hugh twisted in his saddle as they traveled on. He was a touch saddle sore, but there didn't seem much point in mentioning that to any of his brothers.

Sundown found them many miles along the river, where a strip of semi-arid country intruded from the east. There was a gnarled dead tree and the skeleton of a short horse at the spot Frank chose for their camp.

'No cover and no chance of anybody sneaking up on us,' he explained.

Urban acted surprised.

'Are you expectin' Lowe and the others to make a try for us, Frank?'

'If I were him, and I knew somebody was followin' me, I would,' Frank answered. 'Maybe he doesn't know about us yet, but he will, in time. No point in waitin' for him to make his move before we start keepin' sharp, is there?'

Frank paused to indicate the broad furrow of hoof tracks in the sand. They had picked up the outlaw sign five miles or so downstream, and it seemed they were making for the trading post that Boojum, the trapper leader, had mentioned.

'Did you see big Boojum when we mentioned the gang?' Casey said wonderingly. 'Turned white as a sheet, he did. He was sure scared.'

It was silent for a time until Hugh said, 'Like maybe we should be. . . ?'

Frank turned sharply. 'That will be enough of that kind of talk.'

Hugh frowned.

'I will say what I please, Frank.'

'No, you won't . . .' Frank snapped, but bit off his words.

For a moment he sat, looking down at his big brown hands. Then he glanced up and said, 'Sorry, Hugh. As you say, every man has a right to speak. We are all equals here.'

Those simple words went a long way. There had been a growing feeling among the brothers that maybe Frank was starting to ride them a little too hard. To act too much like the officer in charge.

The mood was more relaxed as Frank walked off to stand first watch while the others readied their bedrolls.

Casey joined Frank after a while, to share a final smoke before turning in. Frank stood on the rocky bank of the river with the rifle in the crook of his arm.

To the eyes of the kid, he looked huge and invincible.

'Nice night, huh Frank?'

'Yeah, but there's a bite in the air. Winter's drawin' on, kid,' Frank said.

'Uh huh. Good cuddlin' weather.'

Frank's rare smile showed.

'Thinkin' of that skinny little girl back in Blue Springs Creek, are you?'

'Lucy's not so skinny. I mean, she might not be built like Marlene Welch, but she's real pretty,' Casey noted.

'They are all real pretty until you tie the knot,

Casey. Then they turn mean, and you get to wonder what you ever saw in them.'

'You talk like an old married man,' Casey grinned, relishing the closeness. 'Where did you find out about women, Frank?'

'Books. Where else?'

Casey looked sober.

'Marlene seemed mighty upset to see you go, Frank.'

Frank looked away as he said, 'Women are like that, kid.'

'Lucy says Marlene's still in love with you,' Casey said.

Frank's head angled down. He stared at the river and shifted his weight from one foot to the other.

'Women talk too much, kid. That's another one of their failings. See, your big brother knows all about them.'

'What busted you two up?' Casey asked. 'Ma always said you should have settled down and married Marlene.' He paused to look at his older brother. 'Why didn't you?'

'Ma said that?'

'Many a time. Meant it, too.' Casey shook his head as he answered.

'I guess we just weren't right for each other.' Frank shrugged and threw up his hands.

'I think there's more to it than that.'

'Can you mind your own business, kid?' Frank replied.

'Nope,' Casey grinned. 'Never could, according to

you. What happened, Frank?'

'For some reason, Marlene got the notion that I was too stubborn. That I wouldn't bend, and couldn't be talked out of something once I'd made up my mind. Said she couldn't live with that. Said if I didn't learn to bend, then one day I would snap and that would be it. Curtains for Frank Daniels. Funny critters, these women.'

CHAPTER 6

SHOTS FIRED

The chair splintered when it crashed down on Solly Murdock's hard head, causing his knees to buckle and his eyes to roll in their sockets. But Solly hadn't earned his reputation of being the toughest of all the Murdock gang, friends or cousins for nothing, and as the breed came at him to follow up his advantage, Solly slewed to one side, delivered a chopping blow to the side of his neck, and danced out of harm's way.

'That's the stuff, Solly!' roared Henry Lowe, waving a bottle high. 'Tire him out beatin' up on you. He might have a stroke and you'll win.'

This was meant to goad Solly on, for he was a renowned rough-houser and dearly loved to win. He knew that Henry had money on him, but that wasn't what was important. Winning was everything, but this outsized half breed seemed to have the same attitude.

Solly heaved a table at his adversary, who snatched up a bottle and hurled it, missing Solly and taking out another window.

From the doorway, Trader Wilson watched angrily and anxiously.

At Fort Wilson, where wild men came in and out of the mountains all the time with furs to trade and raging thirsts to quench, brawls were as common as dishwater. Few ever lasted long, and the damage was rarely extensive. This was different. Although both brawlers were brimful of booze, they were both powerful, fierce men who showed no sign of easing up and no consideration whatever for the furnishings.

Wilson was tempted to try and stop the fight. His men were there, ready to help if he gave the word, but the trader hesitated. He wasn't too scared of either brawler, mad and mean as they were. It was the tawny-haired 'trapper' yelling encouragement to the man named Solly that bothered him.

The strangers did not look or act like real trappers. They had hit the post late that afternoon with a fortune in prime pelts from the previous winter and spring.

At first, Wilson had shown some reluctance to handle such a major deal with men he didn't know, but the leader of the band had made it plain there could be trouble if he refused. Wilson named a price, it was accepted, and pelts and cash exchanged hands. The strangers settled down to enjoy themselves. Most of the bunch had gone out to the whores' camp along the river, but the toughest-looking pair had chosen to remain at the post, drinking and raising hell. Eventually they ran up against the fort's meanest customer.

The breed was as big as a house. He had lost his shirt in the ruckus, and his muscular torso gleamed in the fire glow like oiled bronze. There was tremendous power in those heavy shoulders and arms, and he was mean as a rattler as he brushed furniture from his path to close with Solly again.

Solly Murdock's only handicap was a full load of booze. His timing was a touch off and his strength was not quite up to scratch.

Solly took a ferocious elbow smash to the jaw and a stunning punch to the throat. Then he did what any red-blooded man would do when things were looking bad. He went for the eyes with his thumbs.

He found one. The Indian was instantly blinded in his left eye.

He went berserk.

Even Henry Lowe was impressed with the breed's awesome display of savagery as he hurled himself into big Solly. Fists, feet and knees slammed in with a drumbeat sound that shook the room. Solly was head-butted, elbowed, kneed in the groin, spat on, bitten and head-butted again.

Big Solly was down.

The breed had him by the throat and was choking the life out of him.

The crowd cheered this on. No fight could be too rough for these hard-case mountain men. Naturally they were for the local boy, and if Solly had been prepared to go for the eye, then he had to be prepared to accept the consequences.

Solly fought desperately for breath. His lungs were on fire, and a red mist swam before his eyes. He tried for a knee in the groin but missed. His strength was ebbing fast. The one-eyed breed leaned close, his lips split in a wolf grin of triumph which exposed teeth that looked strong enough to crush bone.

The breed's thumbs were probing deeper into Solly's bruised neck. It was plain to everyone that Solly was through. That included Henry Lowe.

Nobody saw him draw, as every eye was fixed on the life and death drama in front of the long bar. The shot crashed through the big room like a bomb going off. A sudden black hole, round, neat and exactly centered, appeared in the breed's forehead. Legs still straddling Solly, he stared at nothing for a long, shocked moment, and then tumbled stiffly to one side.

Choking and wheezing, Solly struggled to a seated position in the stunned silence, worked some saliva around his mouth, and spat in the dead face.

The mob was ready to be outraged until they looked at the gunman. Lowe now had a Colt in each hand, and the only way to describe his expression was eager.

He wanted them to try something. Please, he thought.

Only Wilson dared to offer a word of protest.

'That wasn't rightly fair, mister, what you done.'

Henry Lowe trained one Colt squarely on Trader

Wilson and said, 'Say that again?'

Rugged though he was, the trader went white and dumb. He still did not know who the stranger was, but he was an experienced judge of bad character.

'What a dump!' Lowe sneered, lowering the gun. 'Let's get out of here and go find some real fun, cousin.'

Solly's thick legs were shaky as he followed the broad-backed figure. He couldn't see straight, and he wheezed like a mule with consumption. But he was alive, and for that he was grateful.

'Know what I was thinkin' when the lights was goin' out, Henry?'

'What?'

'That I plan on seein' my wife up north. Imagine what a fool I would have been to let that redguts do me in. . . .' He managed a wheezing chuckle. 'Milly would never forgive me.'

As they mounted up and Henry Lowe glanced back at the lights, he was still half hoping somebody might come after them.

'Seems to me you're slippin' a bit, cousin,' Henry said. Then he slapped his thigh and grinned. 'Dang. Just remembered.'

Big Solly looked confused as he said, 'What?'

'I clean forgot to settle my bets.'

That broke them up, and they galloped off for the river, laughing like maniacs and shooting their guns into the night sky, survivors as they always were.

There was news waiting when they reached the whores' camp. The previous day, Henry Lowe had left a man behind to keep watch. The scout had returned now, with the news that five men were camped on their tracks, following their sign.

'What do we do, Henry?' Solly asked impatiently.

Nobody could ever accuse Henry Lowe of indecisiveness. He turned to his female cousin, Rhonda, and said, 'Kill 'em, of course.'

It was the following night, and the Daniels brothers had made camp just a few miles downstream from Fort Wilson. All was quiet up above as Rhonda Lowe and five of the gang's other henchmen paused to look up at the faint glow of the campfire.

'Greenhorns!' she hissed. 'Who else would light up a beacon to show us where they are? This will be too easy to get any satisfaction out of it. Let's get it over.'

The face of the knoll was thick with shrubbery. It was almost as though nature wanted to assist the killers. The outlaws climbed up the slope with the aid of the undergrowth, like small bears. Six bears. Sending six of his men, or five men and one woman, to deal with the five pursuers showed that Henry Lowe had been in a generous mood. Normally one or two would be regarded as enough.

Rhonda reached the rim first. She was a slender, athletic woman with the characteristic tawny hair and feral green eyes of the Murdocks, she was a cousin, that glittered as she parted a screen of brush to peer towards the campsite. Though she was a woman, she was treated like one of the men and didn't act or dress like a typical woman.

The fire burned merrily. Around it were scattered figures, wrapped in their bedrolls. A line of horses on a picket rope was dimly visible in the background. It was all Rhonda Lowe could do to suppress her contempt for such carelessness. Greenhorns indeed? These jokers were begging to be killed.

Her men were now spread out on either side of the camp, guns glinting in eager readiness.

'No tricky stuff,' Rhonda instructed. 'We just go straight in shootin'. Understand me?'

Heads nodded, and the bad men advanced with no more noise than a moonrise.

A tree to the right moved.

But it wasn't a tree. It was a big man – a very big man – and he was holding a shotgun.

This stunning fact barely had time to register before both barrels of the shotgun erupted in a fierce fireball and Rhonda Lowe fell.

Instantly, other hidden guns erupted in a head numbing roar. Outlaws were tumbling, screaming desperately, trying to fight back. It wasn't easy as the Daniels had the drop on them. They had been lying in wait for more than two hours, ever since Frank had glimpsed the outlaws making their way south along the river.

One man got to put two bullets close to Frank Daniels, but he was quickly shot to pieces by Casey and Urban, firing from different positions.

CHAPTER 7

BLACK STONE FOR THE DEAD

Frank Daniels moved swiftly through roiling tatters of gunsmoke as he glimpsed two dark figures retreating towards the slope. His .45s were fully loaded again, and he was riding a crest of violence. In the uncertain gloom surrounding him men were hurt, dead, fighting and yelling. The chaos made sense of a kind to him.

One of the Murdocks reached the slope first and started down through the brush, hand over hand. Suddenly Frank loomed above him, looking impossibly huge to the descending outlaw. Frank made sure their eyes met before he opened up.

'For my dear mother, Dorothy Daniels!' he roared. Twin Colts belched fire and the man below him gave a faint, weak cry as he plummeted down the slope into the rocks below. The other man instantly gave up trying to climb down and just let himself go. Frank's scorching lead hunted his rolling, frantic figure. He was rewarded by a sharp yell of pain, but the hellion made it to the safety of the rocks and was gone into the brush like a startled jackrabbit.

As Frank swung back into the fray, one of his brothers was hit: Urban had been fighting it out with an outlaw positioned behind a deadfall. He was taken from behind by Rhonda Lowe, who drove four soft-nosed slugs into his back before Frank could get to him.

Rhonda hit the ground with a dead meat thud but managed to survive Frank's shotgun blast and was still alive and moaning as Casey sprang across her to reach Urban's side. But it was already too late for Urban Daniels, and there were tears in Casey's eyes as he swung with gun in hand, meaning to finish off his brother's killer.

Frank's shout held him: 'No, kid! We want that bitch of an outlaw alive to talk!'

So Casey settled for slamming his boot heel into the wounded woman's face, before swinging away to search for more targets.

There weren't any. The battle was over. The tally of bad men was one wounded, one escaped and four shot to death. And there was Urban Daniels staring sightlessly at the sky.

They buried Urban where he had fallen, using saddle shovels to scrape out a grave among the trees and stones. To clear the burial site, they dragged three outlaw corpses away and tossed them down the vine-covered slope where their companion lay.

Thin moonlight filtered down as Frank stood bareheaded, reading from Hugh's bible. They could not believe that their brother Urban was dead. Now there were only four of them.

They had cost the enemy dearly, but four dead scum did not go anywhere near making up for the loss of Urban.

'All he ever wanted was to drift,' Hugh said afterwards. 'I hope they let him do it where . . . where he is now.'

Frank put on his hat and left them standing by the rock-covered grave.

He approached the wounded prisoner with a thin strip of piano wire taken from his saddle-bags in his hands. Rhonda Lowe made a feeble attempt to brush the big hands away as they reached for her, but the effort was in vain. The outlaw woman found herself jerked into a seated position by the wire now tightly encircling her neck.

'Easy, Frank. I believe that outlaw is a woman,' said Virgil.

Frank spat. 'This is no woman, no matter what she looks like.' Frank turned to Rhonda and leaned close. 'Name!' he demanded.

'Go fry!' Rhonda shot back with hate.

The wire tightened, and Rhonda's eyes bulged. She stared into the bronzed face before her and saw no hint of mercy. She was not a woman of great courage. She signaled frantically, and when the choke wire was eased, she blurted out her name.

'Rhonda . . . Lowe.'

Frank's eyes widened fractionally.

'Wife or cousin?'

'Henry's. . . ? Yeah . . . cousin.'

'And you were one of them, weren't you?' Frank declared.

'W-what? One of who?' Rhonda asked.

'You were at the ranch were our mother was butchered,' Frank said through clenched teeth.

'No . . . no. . . !'

The wire jerked tight.

'Frank! She is a woman, for God's sake,' Virgil said again. 'What would Mom think of you treating a woman like this?'

Frank relaxed the wire.

'Start talking, you low-life, good-for-nothing . . . woman!' Frank growled. 'I want to know where Henry Lowe and the rest of the Murdock Gang are, and where they are heading. How many men are in the gang? I want to know everything, and you are goin' to tell me.'

Rhonda Lowe had always considered herself tough, as tough as any man. Not so much as her cousin, Henry, maybe, but tough enough. She resolved not to say anything more – but by the time Frank Daniels was through with her, she had told them everything she could think of, and was begging for an end to her agony. Her wounds were not of the type she could recover from.

Frank took a moment, pulling away from the hands of Virgil who knew what Frank was thinking of doing, and finally decided to grant her last wish.

Almost daintily, he looped the piano wire around the woman's neck. The wire cut deeply into the skin with his first vicious twist. Rhonda Lowe's body leapt like a convulsing fish on the end of a line. Frank held his grip remorselessly as Virgil and Casey turned away until the fish stopped struggling and flopped back to earth, floundering and dying.

With his brothers watching now in ashen-faced silence, Frank held the pressure for a further half minute to make sure. Then he released the wire and put it in his pocket. At the same time, he took out a small black stone.

Frank Daniels dropped the stone on the dead woman's stomach.

'Daniels?' Henry Lowe looked perplexed. 'Is that name supposed to mean something to me?'

The survivor of the bloody battle in the south, a mean-faced Murdock Gang member – Honus McCord – with snaggled teeth and half an ear shot away, had to take another slug of rye before he could reply.

'I dunno, Henry, but that is what the big fella said afore he blasted Zeke: "For my dear mother, Dorothy Daniels!" That's what he said. Then he damn near blew Zeke's head offen his shoulders. . . .'

'Yeah, we heard all of that the first time you told us,' Henry snapped. His eyes were frosty as he stared at his cousin. 'Daniels. . . .'

'Blue Springs Creek, Henry.' It was bad old Uncle Birch Murdock who spoke up. 'Daniels was the name of that old lady you went to when you was lookin' for horses.'

Henry Lowe turned to face his uncle, one of the founders of the gang.

'Are you sure of that, old man?'

'Certain sure. I lined up the raid for you, remember?'

With a nod, Henry began moving around the campfire, watched by a pack of silent outlaws. Murdock's Gang was well accustomed to pursuit, but not to heavy losses. Judging by the survivor's account of the ambush, they had lost heavily. They were waiting for him to tell them what they should do about it, what they should feel, what they should think.

'Daniels?' Henry Lowe muttered. 'Five of 'em . . . huh?' He stopped before Honus McCord. 'And one of 'em was a really big man, you say?'

'Big, Henry, big.'

Henry scratched his head. 'As big as me?'

Honus McCord shook his head. 'Bigger.'

Again it was Uncle Birch Murdock who interrupted.

'That handle, Frank Daniels, that rings a bell with me, nephew. Seems I heard him spoke of from time to time. You know? Like he might be somethin' special.'

'He will be especially dead before he gets to be any

older and bigger,' Henry Lowe promised, turning to Honus McCord again. 'How long do you figure it would take us all to get back to the place you ran away from?'

There was a chill note of censure in Henry Lowe's words. Honus McCord swallowed uneasily.

'Maybe two hours. . . .'

'We cain't go back, Henry.'

The man who spoke was big Solly Murdock, cousin to the survivor and Henry Lowe's long-time gang member. But even Solly could not tell the leader what he could or could not do.

'Solly, shut your mouth or I will shut it for you.'

Henry Lowe was mad; it was a long time since he had been so mad. What had happened downstream had taken the shine off the success of the big fur raid. All he wanted right now was the chance to even accounts with these Daniels.

'I'm only thinkin' of Milly, cuz,' Solly said.

Henry opened his mouth to retort, but then did not. He had forgotten that Solly had received word at Fort Wilson that his wife was seriously ill up at Cibola Hills. Henry had agreed to take the gang to their hideout up near Cibola Hills right away, so that Solly might visit his Milly. He wouldn't do this for any other man, but big Solly was special.

'Damn!' Henry snapped. Then he shrugged and said, 'All right, we'll go north as we agreed.'

'Thank you, cuz,' Solly replied with sincere gratitude.

He was humbly grateful. He was a giant of a man

and a mad-dog killer, but with Henry Lowe, he was unfailingly deferential. Henry Lowe was a man who scared everyone, even his own father.

'But I will send some boys back to take care of these Daniels brothers,' Henry announced. 'Bad enough having old Blythe trackin' us from border to border without somebody else chasin' us for three hundred miles!' The calculation seemed to aggravate him even farther. 'Gila,' he said to the wolf-faced cousin who came closest to himself in lethal ability, 'pick out a bunch of the boys right away, and. . . .'

He stopped when he saw his uncle shaking his grizzled head. 'What's the matter with you now, old man?'

'You are dividing your forces, Henry,' Uncle Birch counselled. 'No good military commander ever does that. You have said so often enough yourself.'

'Judas Priest! We have lost men down there! We could even have lost Rhonda! You remember her, don't ya?'

The old man looked grim and solemn. 'I kinda figure we have already lost her.'

Doc, and two more of Henry's cousins, looked shocked at the old man's declaration.

'That a crazy thing to say, Birch,' Doc protested. 'Rhonda's harder to kill than any man I've ever known.'

'I am just goin' by what we have heard,' Uncle Birch defended. 'Tex here says these Daniels brothers was waitin' for 'em and had the knoll all staked out. They opened up like it was back to Shiloh with all the fences down.' He shrugged. 'He saw two of our boys die, and he said the shootin' stopped not long after he rode off. To me, that means the fight was over and the ambushers carried the day.'

He paused to nod to Henry.

'If you have lost one brother tonight, why risk losin' another?'

There was a war going on inside Henry Lowe. He had fought the same battle before. It was conflict between his natural ferocity and his canny, tactical brain. The main reason his gang had survived so long was due to Henry's cool head in a crisis and his ability to think and plan.

This trait finally manifested itself again now.

'All right,' he said tightly. 'I will just send a scout back to check on Rhonda, and we will keep on to Cibola Hills. We will take care of these Daniels brothers later, if they are still around later.' He shook a finger at Solly. 'And don't you forget you owe me one.'

'What you say, Henry,' Solly replied.

CHAPTER 8

PAY THE TOLL

Rain sluiced against the trail-house windows, a cold and sleeting rain that carried on its breath the chilling promise of early snow. The heavy downpour had wiped out all tracks and forced the brothers to seek sanctuary in the trail house. Leaning on the plank bar with a shot glass in his hand, Frank showed no signs of dejection.

'We don't need tracks,' he was saying. 'We know where they are headed.' He took a slug of warming whiskey. 'Cibola Hills.'

His brothers did not seem to share his confidence. Urban's death still hung heavily upon them. They had killed one of their mother's murderers, but they had lost one of their own in the process. Casey stared into his glass while Virgil kept glancing out of the window at the trail, like he was wishing he was on his way back home.

'How far to Cibola Hills?' Hugh asked the seedy bartender and learned that it was two days ride due north of their current location.

'You'll be lucky not to run into snow up there in Wyoming,' the old man warned. 'I can feel it in my joints.'

'Hell,' Frank mocked, 'that means we'll have to turn back. Snow!'

'I guess it would still be warm in Missouri,' Virgil remarked.

'Missouri,' Casey echoed. 'Sounds kind of strange just to say it now, doesn't it?'

Frank stared into each of his brother's faces, slowly moving from one to the next.

'You boys wouldn't be runnin' out of steam by any chance, would you?'

The brothers all said or at least mumbled, 'No.'

They insisted that there was still plenty of steam, but they were not overly convincing to Frank.

'Well, if you are, there is the door,' Frank said, coming to his full height. 'We are not in the army, and no man's here because he has to be. Go if you want to.'

They looked at him, and he had never seemed taller. He had been through all they had, but he looked untouched by it all. Last night, by the river, they had seen him in action as never before, an implacable force with twin guns dealing death. It was Frank who had sighted the approaching enemy, had set up the ambush and was responsible for their victory. If they had been a little sickened by the way

78

he had dealt with Rhonda Lowe, they had no diffi-culty rationalizing his actions in the light of what they were doing, and especially, why.

Whether Casey, Hugh or Virgil were losing some of their original wrath was not overly important at that moment. What was important was that by quit-ting now, they would be letting Frank down, and in a way, even failing the memory of their dear mother.

When Frank rode off an hour later, his three sur-viving brothers were at his side.

The journey to Cibola Hills occupied two days. They neither saw nor heard anything of their quarry.

On their arrival, they rented a cottage in the river town. While his brothers rested and recovered from ten days of hard travel and danger, Frank Daniels took a walk downtown, to the Dirty Shame Saloon. He proceeded to play the drunk and told anyone who cared to listen that he was on the dodge, and no better than he should be.

Cibola Hills was a tough area and a town with no law, where close-mouthed men minded their own business and strangers were treated warily. But Frank was a patient man when he had to be, and adept at getting people to talk. He continued to play the fool and treated the bar to drinks. Every now and then he slipped in a word or two of sympathy about a 'young woman hereabouts who, they tell me, is dyin' of the fever.'

'That would be Milly Murdock,' one of the saloon's drinkers affirmed.

Once the name Murdock was given air, patient

Frank did not find it hard to slip the name 'Lowe' into general conversation.

Even so, it was getting on towards night before his free booze had loosened tongues sufficiently for them to talk that Cibola Hills was more fearful than admiring of the outlaw band, and that most citizens were none too proud to have the wife of one of the bunch's most notorious members as a resident.

'Milly Murdock is a nice enough lady . . . or was,' a man confided, already putting the woman into the past tense. 'But her husband is nothin' more or less than a butcher.'

'How right you are,' Frank slurred.

Solly Murdock was one of the five. Four now. Rhonda Lowe was dead with a black pebble on her chest. The Daniels brothers intended that Solly Murdock would be the next to go.

Frank burped and gazed at the drinker with what appeared to be blurred eyes.

'But surely those outlaws never bother you good folk hereabouts?' he asked. 'I mean, they are wanted from one end of the country to the other. They wouldn't dare, would they?'

'Oh, they have been here,' he was told. 'Not often, but often enough. So as big Solly can visit with Milly, you understand?'

Frank had already figured that. He put on a disbelieving look.

'Are you tellin' me those outlaws would dare show their faces here in this town?'

The drinker shook his head, and it was then that

Frank heard a local rumor that the Murdock Gang had a hideout someplace west of town, in the sprawling Cibola Hills the town had been named for.

The kid was curious all right.

'You're not goin' out tonight, are you, Frank?' he demanded as Frank took his mackinaw off the elkhorn rack in the corner. 'Hell, a goddamn fish would drown out there.'

Rain hammered on the iron roof. It spilled from overflowing guttering and sluiced down the drains. This was the worst night a man might encounter in six months – and Frank Daniels loved everything about it.

He was calm and casual as a man could be as he shrugged into the heavy weather coat that made him look as big as a house. Smile creases showed at the corners of his eyes as he took down his Stetson and knocked it into shape with the heel of his hand.

'Got me a date to take my mind off Urban, kid,' he said. His eyes went distant. 'You should see her. Hair the color of cornsilk, eyes like a Utah lake in summertime. . . .' He chuckled. 'Well, you get the general idea, I reckon.'

There was no answering smile from Casey.

'You ain't seein' no female,' the youngest Daniels brother accused. 'Why are you lyin' to me, Frank?'

Frank's smile disappeared. He fitted his hat to his head and gave the boy a flinty-eyed look.

'Anybody ever told you that you talk too damn much sometimes, kid?'

81

Casey shook his head. 'Mainly you.'

'Don't you go on gettin' sassy now. I'm old enough to be. . . .'

'Yeah, you've told me that before. Old enough to be my grandfather.'

Frank's face showed surprise. 'Grandfather? Father, that is.'

'Who cares? You are old. I'm young, and you are lyin',' Casey stood firm.

Frank nodded to himself. He knew what Casey's game was. He was trying to goad him into revealing what he was up to. He would not get angry with the boy. Not tonight. There would be anger all right, but it would not be directed against any one of his brothers.

He clapped the boy on the shoulder.

'Get some rest, Casey. We've got a big day tomorrow.'

'Let me come with you, Frank?' Casey pulled away from the shoulder clap, then added, 'Please?'

'Sorry, kid.' Frank could not risk his young brother.

'It is that risky?'

'I didn't say anything about risks. I just don't want you to tag along, is all.'

'You missed your callin', brother,' Casey flared, flushed with disappointment. 'You should have been an attorney, like Hugh. You are a natural liar.'

Frank just grinned and went out, the freezing rain beating against him as he heeled the door closed. Lights from the stables reflected in the pools of water as he went down the steps. Beyond the lights, the night was black with the storm approaching, but he knew what he was doing and where he was going.

The liveryman watched him curiously as he saddled the dark brown thoroughbred. 'Must have a set on yourself goin' horsebackin' on a night like this, big feller!'

At another time, Frank Daniels might had told the fellow to mind his own business. But not tonight. He felt too good.

'I'm the restless kind,' he said, swinging up. 'You know how it is?'

'No, I sure don't,' the liveryman said with a shrug. 'Adios, then.'

The man stood scratching his gray thatch as Frank rode out. Then he closed the doors, cutting off the light.

Frank Daniels rode alone into the darkness.

Just how he liked it.

The weather was just as foul up in the Cibola Hills as on the flats. The great plains sloped east from the Rocky Mountains, extending south from Canada and covering the eastern parts of Wyoming. Much of it was short-grass prairie land, with the Cibola and Black Hills being the major exceptions. It wasn't going to stop Solly Murdock from riding, either. Henry said it was all right for him to go visit his dying wife, just so long as he was careful. The outlaws hadn't seen any sign of pursuit around the area, but they could not afford to be too careful.

Big Solly Murdock was not afraid. Although a long way from being the smartest man in the gang, he was one of the strongest and meanest, for sure. The cussedness in his make-up seemed to spring from some deep physical well. When his anger was up and the blood running hot, he was as dangerous as a runaway. He could be emotional on occasions, and that was his mood tonight as Uncle Birch Murdock walked with him as far as the cave where the horses were hidden. Solly was fond of his wife. She was one of the few people he knew who did not believe he belonged in a cage.

'She'll come through,' Uncle Birch assured him, his face a mass of wrinkles in the lantern light as Solly saddled up. 'You'll see. And don't you stay with her too long, hear me? It ain't safe for any of us to be wanderin' around on our lonesome until we deal with them Blue Springs Creek pilgrims.'

Solly did not even hear him. His thoughts were with his wife, Milly.

'You listenin' to what I'm saying to you, Solly?' Uncle Birch asked.

Solly nodded and then muttered, 'Sure.'

'You be careful,' Uncle Birch Murdock said as he shook his head in Solly's direction.

Solly turned his big, beefy face towards the older man.

'Nobody better mess with me tonight, Birch. If they do, I am as likely to rip their guts out and feed 'em to the fish in the river.'

The bad old man chuckled. He liked that sort of

84

talk. He understood it. Violence and crime were the cornerstones of his existence. The curious thing was the fascination they still exerted over him despite his years.

'Hell, I should not be a-frettin' about you,' Uncle Birch said. 'On your way and say howdy to Milly.'

Once under way, Solly began to relax some. He took a heavy plug of dark chewing tobacco from an inside pocket, bit off a big chunk and mashed it with powerful yellow teeth. That was better, he thought. A man could get too tense without tobacco or whiskey at times to settle the nerves.

Coming out of the hills that were seemingly between the eastern and western mountains, Solly eyed several relatively flat basins with gray curtains of rain sluicing over a wind-tossed landscape; the massive outlaw headed for Bridge Road, which would take him across the toll bridge and thence to Cibola Hills. The toll bridge was the only way across the river when the waters were up.

Munching on his plug of tobacco, his floppy black hat tugged down over his face for protection, Murdock rode along in a cocoon of warmth, inside layers of clothes topped off by a glistening slicker. To keep from fretting about his ill wife, Solly allowed his mind to touch on the ambush.

His stubbed lips twisted in a sneer at the thought of the Daniels. Anybody who figured they would ever get the better of the Murdock Gang had another think coming. Henry Lowe, since his takeover as leader of the gang, and the rest of his followers, would still be thriving after all the lawmen, bounty hunters and outraged civilians had turned up their toes.

The Bridge Road was deserted, as expected. Water ran off it in furrowing streams. Occasionally, lightning shimmered and flickered above, revealing the river.

Soon Murdock could hear the roar of the water in the gloom ahead. Then he glimpsed the dim light of the toll booth and felt in his pockets for change. It used to be five cents. He would not be surprised if it had gone up. It had been that long since he had been home.

As he approached the booth, he could make out the silhouette of the toll man ahead.

What a job, Solly thought. Cooped up in a booth hardly big enough to swing a cat, with the rain pouring down and probably no more than half a dozen customers all night long. Compared to that, riding the owl hoot was paradise.

Solly Murdock whistled through his teeth to alert the man. The booth door opened and Solly reined in, offering the coins.

'How much?'

The toll man did not reply, just fixed him with what Solly Murdock thought was a queer look. The toll man was very big, with shoulders like a barn door. His face was bronzed deeply, and his square jaw was like a rock. Solly thought vaguely that dull, inactive work did not look like it was doing the man any harm.

Then the toll man extended his hands towards him, but not to take his money. Instead, Solly saw that the man was holding out a leather photograph case, opened. The light fell on it, and Solly saw the photograph: an elderly woman with kind, warm features. She was gray-haired and smiling in the photograph.

Familiar.

The elderly woman they had killed in Missouri.

The Daniels!

In that blinding moment, before he could even move, big Solly Murdock knew that he was dead – for the shaved end of a second, his mind ticking along with astonishing clarity and calm, recognizing the inevitable, almost as though ready to accept his fate.

Then primitive reflex took over, and an animal cry tore from Solly Murdock's throat as he tore at his slicker, trying to reach his holstered pistol.

But Frank Daniels pulled his .45 and shot Solly in the chest. He shot him again in the neck as Solly swayed in the saddle, no longer trying to get his pistol. The horse was leaping away in fright, and the outlaw was falling from the saddle.

Miraculously, Solly Murdock was still alive. There was so much primitive power in his big body that he was actually able to push his torso up out of the mud and lift his ashen face to Frank, trying to say something.

Looming gigantically above him, Frank Daniels fired until the huge body lay face down under the uncaring rain.

Frank produced a small black stone and dropped it on the corpse. The water pooling around the body was turning pink in the light from the toll booth.

Solly Murdock would be searching for water coins to pay the toll across the River Styx now.

CHAPTER 9

A STUDY IN MURDEROUS FURY

Henry Lowe kept prodding the huge corpse as though unable to comprehend that Solly Murdock was really dead. Nobody else gathered in the old barn had any trouble accepting the fact. They had seldom seen anybody so shot to hell as the former strong man of the bunch. Half his skull was missing, and only half his face was left. Just looking at the corpse, one could feel the fury that had gone into the killing. Big Solly Murdock had not been so much assassinated as obliterated.

Finally, Henry stepped back from the bench with an expression of disgust, like he was sore at Solly for allowing himself to get killed in this manner.

The Daniels!

Nobody attempted to stop Henry Lowe now, as he

ordered the entire gang into their saddles. Not only would nobody have dared, but none wanted to. Suddenly the Daniels brothers loomed large as a real threat to the band.

The scouts whom Henry had sent to Cibola Hills the moment he was informed of Solly's death had, as usual, done their work stealthily and well. They reported to Henry that four strangers had rented the Cosgrove house on Beech Street, and Tex Murdock confirmed that their description matched the men he had seen at the ambush who had taken the life of several of the gang members, including Rhonda Lowe.

Another rider hammered up as they prepared to go. The outlaw brought the news that Milly Murdock had passed away overnight, without knowing that her husband had been killed two miles from home.

Henry's face was a study in murderous fury. It seemed in his fevered imagination that everything and everybody around him was being tainted by this tribe from Missouri. He found it hard to believe that a bunch of amateurs had done him more harm than all the powerful posses that had hunted him over the years.

Their time was numbered, he vowed. There was no subtlety or stealth in Henry Lowe's thinking now. The Daniels were bugs, and he was ready to use a mallet to mash them.

Quitting the hills, the outlaw gang galloped like Cossacks over the frozen plain towards the town.

*

Casey Daniels was pulling on his riding boots.

'Two down, Frank! Two down and three to go. Who said that nobody could take that scum outfit? We are doin' it in style too, huh?'

'Sure, sure, kid,' Frank replied impatiently from the doorway. 'Get a move on, kid, we don't have all day you know.'

'Hey,' Casey protested, 'it is not even sun-up yet. What's the rush?'

Breath fog gusted from Frank's mouth as he turned his head. They would not see the sun today. Freezing northers had blown away the rain, and the leaden shape of the clouds threatened snow. Outside, Virgil and Hugh were saddling the horses. They were taking up the hunt again, bright and early. Frank predicted that Solly Murdock's death would stir the gang to flight, retaliation or panic. He meant to be mobile and ready when they moved.

'You are worse than a woman,' Frank chided. 'I'll bet that girl of yours back home doesn't take as long as you do to get dressed.'

Casey chuckled. The death of another outlaw had cheered them all and helped them push their brother's death into the background.

'Lucy? Heck, she takes no time at all gettin' ready. Know why that is, Frank? She does not even think she is pretty. Can you believe that?'

Frank said dryly. 'I have seen prettier women.'

Casey shied a boot at him. Frank was actually grinning as Hugh came up the steps, blowing into his hands.

'Horses are ready, Frank. How are we holdin' for ammunition?'

'We'll have to stock up later today, when the stores are open. That is, unless we are on the chase.'

'Are we heading out to the hills around here now?' Hugh asked.

'Yeah. The fact that Murdock was on that road proved they are holed up out there in the hills for sure,' Frank noted.

'I hope they stand their ground, Frank. I would like to face them down and finish this once and for all,' Hugh added.

'I wouldn't bank on that, Hugh. I have never met an owlhoot yet with any real guts when the fight was carried to him. I would not be surprised if those so-called badmen are makin' far apart tracks for the next state right now.' Frank turned his head. 'Casey!'

'Yeah, I know,' Casey replied. 'Get a wiggle on.'

'Well, do it and quit talkin' about it then,' scolded Frank.

'Needs a mammy, that kid,' Hugh said with an affectionate smile.

Frank nodded. 'I couldn't agree more.'

Hugh sobered. 'Are you feelin' all right, Frank? I mean after last night?'

Frank thrust his big hands deep into his pockets. 'Sure, I'm all right. Why shouldn't I be?'

Hugh eyed his older brother. 'The killing doesn't bother you?'

Frank's eyes were on the house opposite.

'You get . . .' he paused. 'I'm used to it. That's all.'

Hugh was tempted to go farther, but he did not. The air of mystery surrounding Frank might be less dense now than two weeks back, but there was still a lot about him they didn't know. The shooting, for instance. Attorney Hugh had always known his older brother was handy with a gun, but not until now did he realize that Frank was exceptionally good with a gun. They were operating in the big league now, and Frank wasn't just holding his own, but was setting the pace for the rest of them.

'It'll be good to get back home, Frank.'

'Huh? Oh yeah, sure, Hugh.' Frank pointed across the street. 'Now, what do you think is ailing that varmint? Has he got a flea in his ear, or do you think he is just seized up from the cold?'

Hugh turned to look. Their neighbor had emerged to stand on his front porch, peering past the willows towards the main street. He stood motionless with head cocked to one side, hand cupped to his ear.

'Looks like he is listenin' to something,' Hugh commented. He glanced towards town. 'Can you hear anything, Frank?'

Frank could not. Due to the line of heavy willows along their street, the sound coming faintly from the main street had not reached their cabin yet, although it had caught the attention of the sharp-eared old man across the road. The man suddenly straightened up and blinked. Now he was not only hearing a strange sound in Cibola Hills' early morning, but he could see the cause of it.

He started in waving his skinny arms and calling to somebody inside the house. Above the sound of his dry old voice, carrying sharply over the frozen air, the Daniels suddenly heard the sound.

It was the roar of a flooded river, but somehow different. It was the racing drumbeat of many hoofs. The instant he heard the noise, Frank knew he had made an error in judgment. It was as if he knew what was pouring down Main Street before he even saw it.

'Inside! Hurry!' he bellowed, seizing Hugh by the shoulder and heaving him through the door. He whipped out a Colt and beckoned imperiously to Virgil. 'Run, goddammit! They are comin'!'

Virgil didn't need any second urging. He was diving past Frank as the first wild rider showed beyond the willows. It was Henry Lowe himself.

Frank instantly recognized the outlaw leader from the older posters at the Blue Springs Creek jailhouse, but the main difference between the real man and the picture was his size. Lowe was much bigger than he had imagined. Henry Lowe sat his saddle with the grace of an Indian and used the rifle tucked under his arm with bewildering skill. The shot he ripped off at a racing run clipped the doorframe mere inches from Frank's head.

Instantly, Frank spun inside and kicked the door shut. A man could get killed out there, even a Frank Daniels.

He darted to a window and knocked the glass out with his gun barrel, hoping to get a bead on Henry Lowe. The momentum of Lowe's charge had carried the outlaw leader some distance past the house where the brothers were now holed up, while those coming behind came surging directly towards him across the ice-slicked grass.

As he threw up twin Colts and fired, shaking the building with the thunderclap of the shot, Frank made an impressive sight with his head tilted back, six-shooters flaming, everything about him defiant and unafraid. His brothers felt they were seeing him as he really was, the man of the gun facing his foes. The legend that all talked about.

Then all four brothers were totally absorbed in throwing lead. Two racing riders went down, but the others kept coming. The cabin shook to the impact of lead.

CHAPTER 10

A TIME TO KILL

The snow came about noon, and it came on suddenly. It swirled over the hills and the town of Cibola Hills, whitening the roof of the Beech Street house where the Daniels brothers were holed up, and the blood-spattered grass surrounding the house. It settled wetly on the besieging Murdock Gang, forever replenishing itself. Within an hour the snow had covered the ground and brought to the whole countryside a silent and stealthy cold that afforded a stark contrast to the hot violence holding Beech Street in its grip.

Frank Daniels lurched to his feet and hobbled to the fireplace to grab an iron poker to use as a makeshift cane.

'Don't look at me,' he barked as he saw the eyes of his brothers on him. 'Watch the damn outlaws!'

His brothers – Virgil, Hugh and Casey – switched

their attention to the bullet-shattered windows, leaving Frank to limp towards the doorway of the first bedroom in the house. His pants' leg was soaked in blood. Frank didn't know where the slug that had slammed into his thigh about two hours prior had come from. He kept ripping up sheets to use as strapping, but he was still losing blood.

'Don't waste lead, kid,' he cautioned Casey, the youngest, positioned hard by the front door of the house. 'Make every shot count. You hear me? We are gettin' mighty low on ammunition.'

'And they know it, Frank,' Virgil noted.

Casey's narrow face was pale, his eyes unnaturally bright. The ambush at the river had been dangerous stuff, but this was desperate. There was no sign of the siege being lifted, and there was little hope they would get out of this alive. Every now and then they would hear Henry Lowe urging his men on, reminding them of lost family members and the virtue of vengeance. Not a towner had been sighted since the siege began. Cibola Hills was watching avidly but wanted no part of the fight. Who could blame them?

'They know we are losin', boys: that was what they know,' Frank said through gritted teeth.

Casey ducked as a bullet zipped through the window and flattened itself with jarring impact against the far wall. He drew a bead on a dim shape and gently squeezed the trigger.

'That's the way you do it, kid,' Frank said, moving on. 'We got to make it last.'

'Until what?' smudge-faced Hugh muttered, but

nobody heard him.

Reloading his rifle, Hugh was thinking of Kansas, with sun on the wheat fields and him in his buggy, heading for a fight – but the kind lawyers hold in courthouses. Not this kind. Not the kind where men would end up dead.

There were two dead outlaws outside, one on the grass in front of the house and the second in the alley. The snow was slowly covering them both. It continued to fall, pretty and silent, a gentle touch on a brutal day.

In the side room, Frank sat on a chest by the window to reload his rifle. He had a view of the next-door house and portion of the side street. The outlaws had taken over the houses on either side and across the street. Warm and reasonably safe there, all they had to do was keep the Daniels pinned down and wait for them to run out of bullets.

The defenders' prospects did not look good.

Frank examined his leg. He was lucky the slug had missed the bone, but it was a serious wound nonetheless. By tomorrow, the leg would be the size of an Ozark ham, and maybe the wound would be heading for infection.

If he and his brothers lived to see tomorrow, that is.

Movement flickered in a window opposite. Frank lifted his rifle to his shoulder and waited. The movement was not repeated. The enemy had grown cautious. They knew the Daniels must soon run out of ammunition. All the outlaws had to do was wait.

'Frank!'

It was Virgil, calling from the next room.

'Yeah, Virg?'

'I can see one of the sons of bitches on top of the feed store!'

Frank sighed. 'Well, shoot him off it then.'

'I might hit him, but I'm guessin' you would be certain to hit him.'

'I think you will do just fine,' Frank urged.

'Maybe,' Virgil muttered, 'but I had best leave him to you.'

'Why?'

Frank's leg throbbed. For a minute or two, he wanted to just sit quietly on this old chest and rest up.

Virgil's face appeared around the bullet-ridden wooden doorjamb.

'On account of you don't miss, Frank.'

Frank stared down at his rag-swaddled thigh for a long moment before rising. Going through, he let Virgil point out the target. The roof-climbing man was an outlaw all right, a barely visible figure sprawled atop the grain store, working a repeating rifle.

'Easy pickins for you, Frank, huh?'

'Maybe . . .' was all Frank said in response.

Frank was lining up his rifle as Hugh appeared in the front-room doorway. The two brothers watched him silently as he took aim. Even though Hugh and Virgil were fully aware they might not survive, they were watching closely, learning and absorbing from their older brother. They rated Frank as the best.

What the rat-faced sniper thought at that moment was not known. A good guess would be that he was figuring he was next to invisible, up there on his roof with the curtaining snow falling. He was almost certainly thinking in terms of bagging somebody with his repeater Winchester, when Frank Daniels gently squeezed his trigger.

The bullet took the outlaw in the head. It did not kill him outright, however. Instead, the shot jerked him to his feet to do a crazy jig on the roof, spinning and flapping his arms until Casey fired from the front room and sent him spinning from sight.

The response was a furious volley of lead from the hidden killers encircling the house. The guns thundered and stormed for maybe a minute before Henry Lowe was able to make himself heard.

'I said save your lead!' he roared.

'But they got Brad, Henry,' a rifleman protested adamantly.

'Who cares? The idjit was askin' for it, climbin' up there.'

The shooting eased off abruptly and then ceased altogether.

'That pilgrim is all heart,' Frank commented, climbing to one knee with some effort. 'And you boys think I'm tough on you! Jeez.'

The remark was meant to relieve the tension, and it succeeded. Casey, Hugh and Virgil exchanged smiles, something none of them thought was possible after the death of Urban.

A long silence was broken by Henry Lowe's voice

again: 'Hey, you Daniels in there? You know you are goin' to all die, right? Make it easy on yourselves and just give up!'

Frank waited, rifle at the ready. They saw figures moving behind curtained windows, but there was no chance of getting in a decent shot at any of them.

'Frank Daniels!'

Henry's voice sounded like a rifle sound. 'The one who killed Solly Murdock. Give me a look at you, Daniels. You are a no good, good for nothin' mongrel, sir. I spit at the mention of your name, Daniels.'

Frank did not hesitate with his reply. 'I will do a deal, scumbag!' Frank spoke calmly. 'You show yourself, and then I will show myself.'

Just the sound of Frank's voice was enough to set on edge Henry Lowe's always edgy temper.

'You figure your momma got it rough, Frank Daniels? Judas Priest, what happened to her was paradise alongside what I have in store for you and your brothers.'

The head and shoulders of an outlaw appeared above a slat fence by the house. Behind Frank, Virgil rose impulsively, swinging up his pistol.

'Frank! I can't miss!'

There was panic in Frank's face as he swung from the hips. '*Get down . . .*' he began but got no farther. Virgil was unaware that a window directly behind him silhouetted him clearly. There were marksmen in the outlaw ranks, and several of them opened up before Frank could drag his brother down.

All three brothers knew that Virgil had been killed, just by the way he was hurled backwards, looking down disbelievingly at the ruddy holes in his chest.

His collision with the wall shook the house, but his slide to the floor was only a whisper of sound against the boards and the echoing gunshots.

As Casey and Hugh leapt to their brother's side, Frank came up off his knee to blast four rapid shots into the building opposite them. As gunshots answered, he sprang to another window, fired, went to another window and fired into a doorway from where Henry Lowe's voice had emanated.

Only then did he drop flat and turn his face towards his surviving brothers.

The kid was crying.

Hugh had aged a decade.

Virgil was dead.

Frank was methodical again as he fingered shells from his belt into his rifle. He had just wasted a lot of bullets, he knew. If he had hit anything, it would have been pure luck. They were running low on ammo, all of them, and he was wasting what he had. Nobody reproved him. It was doubtful that his brothers were even aware of him at that grim moment.

'Get back to your posts,' he ordered.

'Damn you for an unfeelin' bastard!' Casey yelled. 'Can't you see that. . . .'

'Nothin' wrong with my eyesight, kid,' Frank cut in. 'And what I see is two men goin' to pieces before my eyes, and a dog pack outside of hungry wolves

102

gettin' ready to mount a rush and tear us to bits.'

They thought he was just talking. But it was the truth. The outlaws were readying for another assault.

The storming volley that erupted simultaneously from all sides of the besieged house continued for a full, brain-numbing minute before the first figures appeared. They came on howling at the top of their lungs, and that was how two of them met their fates.

Casey and Hugh were slow to man their positions again, but Frank held off the outlaws single-handed, never shooting from one position twice, moving from window to doorway with lightning speed, ignoring a crippled leg and shooting with demonic accuracy.

With the long day dying and the snow continuing to fall, the outlaws maintained the pressure. Spurred on by Henry Lowe's ranting voice, they rushed again and again, only to be driven back each time, while taking heavy toll of the Daniels' ammunition reserves.

Frank had just nine pistol slugs left in his guns when the tide turned.

From somewhere beyond the battle zone, rifles spanged sharply and hoofs clattered with a sharp ring on frozen ground. The bad men howled in confusion as they began to fall. They glimpsed the menacing figures of charging horsemen attacking through the snow.

Nobody called retreat: Henry Lowe and the Murdock Gang simply fled, fighting a rearguard action. A tall and overweight federal lawman led his riders after them, across bloodied snow. As Casey and Hugh Daniels gaped in astonishment, Frank reefed a door open and went charging out, dragging his leg, to join in the rout.

Somehow, as the bad men fought their way to their horses and mounted up, big Frank worked his way ahead of the lawmen. He slid to a halt in a low crouch, shooting one man out of the saddle and clipping another.

From the corner of his eye, he glimpsed a broad-shouldered rider with tawny hair flowing to his shoulders and a .45 in his fist.

Frank dived into the snow as Henry Lowe went by, teeth locked, six shooter still blazing. A combination of poor light and the speed of Frank's spinning roll into a snowdrift prevented accuracy.

By the time Frank rose, the last hellion was out of range.

CHAPTER 11

THE DEAD NUMBERED THIRTEEN

Marshal John Blythe loved his food. Even at times of high drama or deep depression, he could always set himself down before a big platter of vittles and dig into it as though there was no tomorrow.

In the wake of the rout of the outlaws, John Blythe felt – well, hungry. He was, of course, pleased that he had been able to save brave men from certain death, and that he had given Henry Lowe and his Murdock Gang some hurry-up before they got away. But being unable to pursue the gang because of the condition of his horses left him a little dejected, even though his deputies kept cheering him by coming into the hotel with reports on fresh casualties.

The tally stood at seven outlaws since his deputies

had found another man dying of wounds in a back alley under a tree. He had not been able to get away – alive, at least.

Marshal Blythe speared a fat sausage and munched aggressively. Seven, plus the others that the Daniels had killed tallied up to thirteen of the gang killed. Thirteen! He only wished to God he had more men like them, especially big Frank who had virtually fought off the enemy on his own. Too bad the brothers would not be joining him now, when he pushed on after the remnants of the gang, he reflected.

Blythe glanced up from his plate at sounds from the street. Two of the Daniels brothers wearing crêpe armbands rode slowly into view, followed by a buckboard driven by the large one called Frank.

The day was bitterly cold, and the brothers were heavily rugged up, Frank with an Indian blanket over his legs. The big man was pale, but the marshal noted that he sat straight. The hands on the reins were firm and steady.

It took something important to draw Marshal John Blythe away from a half-finished meal, but he rose now to set his hat on his head. Then he went to the rack and shrugged into his greasy sheepskin coat before moving to the double doors.

The Daniels had turned in to the hitch rail for a word with the deputies. Marshal John Blythe threw a half salute as he walked out into the wet falling snow. The Daniels brothers looked much recovered from the previous day's shootout, but there was no mistaking the immense grief they were all suffering.

Marshal John Blythe glanced at the armbands and then said, 'My men tell me you had a funeral this morning?'

All the Daniels nodded in response, and Casey said, 'Virgil's at peace now. Can we leave it to you to guarantee they don't plant any of those vermin in the same graveyard as our brother, Marshal?'

'You have got my word, son,' Marshal Blythe answered sincerely. 'Headin' back to Blue Springs Creek, are you then?'

'It will be a spell before I can sit a saddle,' big Frank conceded reluctantly, and Blythe saw that his face was sheened with sweat. 'I guess I will need some nursin' . . . and maybe my brothers will need time to recover from what happened here.'

'Sensible decision indeed, Mr Daniels.' John Blythe serviced his teeth with a combination toothpick and ear cleaner. His teeth were worn down by a lifetime of heroic performances at the table. 'At least you can rest easy, knowin' I will be continuing the hunt for the dirty hellions who killed your brother. You will hear about it if anything happens, and I sure hope to hell it does.'

'Then our tracks might just cross again, Marshal,' Frank said. 'On the trail, I mean.'

Marshal John Blythe stared.

'I don't understand,' he said with a frown. 'You are giving up on this foolishness now, aren't you?'

It was big Frank's turn to stare in response.

'Give up? What are you talkin' about? We will give

up when they are all dead, and not a moment before. Understand?'

'But you have lost two brothers already, and you are hurt bad yourself,' Blythe protested. 'What is it you want – to keep goin' until you have all been buried by this gang?'

'You are not suggestin' we rely on you to finish the gang for us, are you, Marshal?' Frank Daniels asked coldly.

This was a harsh thing to say to a man who had just saved your life, but Blythe understood. He had been engaged in the full-time pursuit of Henry Lowe and the Murdock Gang for going on three years now, and yet they were still at large – the majority of them, anyways. If the band was in poor shape at the present moment, it was not due to his efforts, but rather to the five men he had blithely dubbed 'amateurs' down in Blue Springs Creek.

Yet he had to say, 'You would be a fool even to think of continuin' this chase, Mr Daniels. I know the Murdock Gang better than you do, especially Henry Lowe. He is alert to you now, and you will never get the jump on him again. And that outlaw is vengeful. It is not beyond the bounds of possibility that he will now come lookin' for you without waitin' for you to chase him again.'

Frank's smile was serious and grim.

'Now that is something I just hope happens, Marshal. Maybe I will put a piece in the papers, tellin' him where to find me.'

Marshal John Blythe realized that the big man

really meant what he said.

Then it hit home.

He knew who Frank Daniels reminded him of. Himself! Not the slow, graying, overweight John Blythe of Cibola Hills, Wyoming, but the young, remorseless manhunter he had once been.

Frank Daniels was the marshal as he had been nearly twenty years ago!

Taken aback by this revelation, the marshal stopped trying to talk the brothers out of their decision. Nobody had ever succeeded in dissuading him from anything he had set his mind to when he was younger. Nor when he was older, either, for that matter, he had to confess. He knew he would still continue to drag his aging body around the West in Henry Lowe's bloodied boot prints, even though he was more acutely aware than ever that there were younger, better men available for the job.

He would keep after this man until one of them was dead. Just like Frank Daniels would.

Marshal Blythe stepped back from the buckboard and saluted once more. 'Take care, gents. And good luck to you.'

Some of the iron left big Frank Daniels' pale and pained face.

'We owe you one, Marshal. We won't forget. You have my word.'

'You could repay me best by staying out of this. Go home,' Marshal John Blythe replied, giving it one last try.

'If I ever give up on this, you will know I am dead,

Marshal,' came the uncompromising answer.

Frank slapped the horse with the reins, and the Daniels were heading for the trail, followed by the admiring eyes of an entire town.

Marshal John Blythe was deeply sad. Sad to think he might never see any of those brothers alive again.

CHAPTER 12

OUT OF THE MOUTH OF BABES

Uncle Birch Murdock was coughing harshly. He had been coughing for damn near two days straight now and showed no sign of letting up. The old bad man had picked up a chill in the Cibola Hills, and he could not seem to shake it off. Of course, being a mean old coot with a rugged image to uphold, he was not about to take good care of himself, either. Nobody could get him to wrap up in front of a roaring fire. His sole concession to pain and lung congestion was to sip continually from a bug jug. The contents brought a flush to his cheek and a tear to his eye whenever he got to thinking of the dead.

Not the gang's dead in general. Just his niece, Rhonda. And Solly Murdock. He had had a lot of time for big Solly. Now both were gone. By hell, what

111

he would not do to have big Frank Daniels hogtied for half an hour!

Uncle Birch coughed again, and Henry Lowe told him to stopper it.

'Just what I always wanted,' Birch said sourly. 'A lovin' boy to look after me when I am ailin'.'

'I don't know which is worse, old man – that death rattle or your flappin' tongue. Put a stop to both of 'em – or I will,' Henry snapped.

Not only Uncle Birch Murdock, but every man present was silent after that. They could read the signals. Henry Lowe was primed to blow. He had never taken defeat well. It was not in his nature. And Cibola Hills had been a defeat, and no mistake. The outlaws had failed to pry the Daniels brothers loose from their house, and then had failed to anticipate the arrival of the lawmen. That added up to failure, no matter how you looked at it.

Henry Lowe would never admit to blame, but he secretly blamed himself for the Blythe incident. In his growing preoccupation with the Daniels, the outlaw had all but forgotten plodding Marshal John Blythe. The outlaw had made Blythe look foolish so often that he expected to do it all the time. After their last run-in, down in the Indian Nations, Blythe was left wandering in the badlands with no idea where the gang had gone.

If Henry Lowe had thought of Blythe at all after that incident, it had been only to picture him floundering around somewhere down South, sniffing around jail houses, dives and backwater hideaways in a vain search for a lead. But Marshal John Blythe had been able to follow the Daniels. They had left pretty clear tracks, and corpses, too. . . .

Henry Lowe leaned from the window of the Cheyenne Hotel and fixed a sour stare on the winter landscape. How he hated the cold! The South called to him, but something else was more insistent. He surveyed deserted railroad yards and acres of empty cattle pens. An urge to ignore common sense or even sanity nagged him to return to Cibola Hills and finish what he had begun. He wanted all the Daniels brothers dead, and he wanted to be the man to kill each and every one of them.

The outlaw was arguing with himself. There was a bank to rob over at Big Horn, and then a clean getaway all the way to the sun-washed Southwest, and then another big job that might net more in one stroke than all their other jobs put together. Excitement, action, success – and sunshine. He wanted it all, and he wanted even more than that. He wanted to flirt with dark-eyed women, and maybe even help the old man of the gang, his uncle, to stop coughing his insides out.

Opposing all this was the almost overpowering compulsion to act like a fifteen-year old punk hard case and head back to Cibola Hills.

Henry Lowe shivered. He had fought this battle before, and if he was lucky enough to live a long life, he would no doubt fight it again and often. He lunged from the overheated building and went trudging through the snowdrifts behind the hotel to allow his brain to cool.

He was without a coat or hat as he stood on a corner, freezing in the icy wind while he thought about the dead family and gang members he had lost. He would miss them, especially big Solly. It made his blood congeal each time he thought of how Frank Daniels had anticipated Solly's movements and waited for him to take the bridge over the river.

Seeing Daniels' face again in his mind's eye, he lived with the certain knowledge that one of them would not make it through the river. That made him realize that at least subconsciously, he had reached his decision. Already he was thinking in the long term, not the impetuous here and now.

Every man in the Murdock Gang was relieved to see the change in him when he returned from his sub-zero walk. He even half apologized to his uncle before announcing that they would push on west, for the bank job, in about an hour's time.

'We are goin' to have us a fine old time down South after that, you and me, Uncle Birch. We'll give those law dogs hell,' he promised with a smile, 'and just you wait until you see the job I got in mind. You will be rich and healthy, and we'll forget the bad things that have happened to us up here.'

'You are a good man, Henry,' Uncle Birch Murdock grinned. 'Would you like some of the special stuff I got hold of, to drink a toast to the South?'

The moonshine Uncle Birch produced was a far cry from the Tennessee bourbon they drank when things went their way, but it was real whiskey with a robust, masculine fire that settled in the stomach in a way to make any man feel good.

Uncle Birch was full of pep and good nature by the time they set out nearly an hour later, but he kept right on coughing, and all through the following week, when they successfully robbed the Big Horn bank.

Then the old hellion took a turn for the worse in a little Colorado cowtown, and they buried him the next day. That was a signal mark of respect from a gang where even a man's best friend could be left to rot where he fell dead.

Henry Lowe, Doc and Gila all took the old man's death especially hard.

Henry put the blame for Uncle Birch's death on the Daniels, and vowed that after just one more job, the gang would be going back to Blue Springs Creek, Missouri.

The quietness of Blue Springs Creek seemed more noticeable than at any time ever before that day. Leaning on a cane, Frank Daniels limped the length of the main street to the empty cattle pens, crossed the street and started back.

No snow had fallen in that part of the country since the brothers' return, and the cold was unrelenting. Frank was still pale, and even though he wore a heavy, wool-lined coat, it was clear that he had lost weight since Wyoming. Blood poisoning from the bullet had set in and he had been laid up for nearly ten days upon his return. He had had a suite at the hotel with the medico calling on him twice a day, and Marlene Welch and Lucy Keller taking turns to nurse him back to health.

Nothing had been heard of Henry Lowe and the Murdock Gang since Cibola Hills. There was a rumor circulating that Lowe and his uncle had both died from wounds sustained in the Cibola Hills siege. Frank, of course, did not buy it. He would not count Henry Lowe dead until he saw the corpse, riddled with his own lead.

Marlene glanced up from her paperwork and saw only one person visible in the chill, rutted street. Her heart was in her eyes as she watched the way Frank Daniels leaned on the cane and swung his right leg. She had seen his pain, nursed him through raging fevers, and calmed him when the nightmares tormented him. He would never know how gentle she had been to him when he was out of his head, and she treasured the intimacy they had shared without his knowledge.

Marlene Welch was storing up memories. She knew what would happen when Frank Daniels was well enough to shed the cane again.

She would be alone . . . alone once more.

At the sound of a quick, light step, she lowered her head and pretended to be engrossed in her work. Lucy Keller appeared at her side. She wore a simple gingham dress with lace at the wrists and throat, looking more like a young schoolmarm than ever.

Lucy could sing like a bird, and the paying customers loved her, but Marlene knew the girl did not belong in a saloon.

'Miss Marlene?' Lucy's voice was tense.

'What is it, honey?' Marlene replied.

'Do you have a minute?' the girl politely asked.

For as long as she could, Marlene continued to stare down at her ledger. She sensed what was coming, and she was not sure of what to say. Marlene was not the only woman in Blue Springs Creek in love with a Daniels, and the feeling between Lucy and Casey had deepened since the brothers' return. The boy was a constant visitor from the spread.

'Miss Marlene?'

With a sigh, Marlene set down her pen and looked out again. The towering figure in the bulky overcoat was leaning against the hitch rail outside Percy Claymore's dry goods store, setting a light to a cigar. She felt for the man, and she was angry, too – angry that she had fallen in love with a man like Frank Daniels.

'What is it, honey?' she finally asked, leaning back and turning her swivel chair.

'Miss Marlene, Casey is in the kitchen eating hot-cakes. . . .'

'He's a growing boy,' Marlene replied. 'Nothing wrong with him eating, is there?'

'No,' Lucy said. 'Please, Miss Marlene, this is no joking matter. What I mean to say is that he just said Frank told him and Hugh to get ready for a trip,

117

maybe a long one. Did you know about that?'

Marlene Welch glanced away as she said. 'I knew they would be going sooner or later.'

'But they can't, Miss Marlene. It was a miracle Casey wasn't killed before. I am not going to stand and watch him ride off again, probably to his death. I won't!'

'Calm down, Lucy. Nobody said they are going to die,' Marlene reassured the girl.

'You are thinkin' the same thing I am!' Lucy accused.

'What do you mean?' Marlene snapped.

'You are not so hard to read as you might think. I've seen you fretting. You know what Frank has in mind, and you are just as fearful as I am, but you don't want to admit it. You don't want Frank Daniels to know how much you worry about him, or how you dread what might happen if they hunt those outlaws again. Don't you see, Miss Marlene? We are both the same. The only difference is that you won't admit it. But I want you to. And I want you to go to Frank and tell him how you love him, and how crazy it would be for him to take Casey and Hugh away again. Will you do it, Miss Marlene? Will you do it for both of us?'

Out of the mouths of babes, thought Marlene Welch. She could not deny the truth of what the young girl said, and she decided quite suddenly that she could not refuse to do as she asked.

It was time to set pride aside and beg for what she wanted, Marlene told herself. And what she wanted most in God's green world was the big man – Frank Daniels.

But most of all she wanted him alive.

CHAPTER 13

REGRETS AND UNFINISHED BUSINESS

With a cigar clamped between his teeth, Frank Daniels paused to look into the mercantile store through washed and gleaming plate-glass windows. The merchant was using this quiet day to take stock. He sighted Frank's big figure, smiled and waved politely. Frank did not return the greeting; he was too busy thinking – lost in thought, as they say.

How could those storekeepers do it? How could they ignore the excitement, uncertainty, color, pleasure and danger of the huge world outside, just to stand behind a counter all day long, drumming fingers on a change mat and forever waiting?

Then he saw the boy. It was the storekeeper's son. He recognized him because they were identical. A gangling kid with a prominent Adam's apple and a pink nose. But a kid, nonetheless. The storekeeper's kid at that. He had that to show for his time on earth. . . .

It was more than Frank had.

Frank turned his back and moved on. He frowned. Surely he wasn't beginning to envy bloodless store-keepers and standing behind a counter all day? Was he?

It was one of the consequences of his illness, he decided, possibly caused by blood loss and medica-tion. That made sense to him. And he was quite sure that he knew the cure for it: it was called action. And Frank Daniels was, after all, a man of action.

He deliberately stepped off the porch, to test his leg. It stood up reasonably well, all things considered – it gave him some pain, but there was no loss of function. Frank drew in a deep breath of cold air to fill his barrel chest. The Indian Nations, he was thinking. The rumors put the Murdock Gang and Henry Lowe somewhere in the Indian Nations. Plenty of sunshine and warmth down there. A man would heal fast in that kind of weather.

'Howdy, Frank.'

The sheriff, Drew Hancock, had emerged from the tobacco store, peeling the wrapper off a chunk of plug. The man's manner was respectful. The Daniels' achievements in the north were already taking on the aura of legend, and everyone was proud of them, even if many were shocked by the deaths of Urban and Virgil.

Frank just nodded in response, still deep in his own thoughts. It was time, he was telling himself. He was ready.

'Good to see you up and about, lookin' chipper again, Frank,' the sheriff declared.

Frank nodded once again, then said, 'Thanks, Sheriff.'

The lawman drew nearer as he added, 'Heard the latest?'

Frank's face showed life. 'Tell me.'

'It is official. The old man, Birch Murdock, is indeed dead. Just him, though. The rest of the bunch disappeared down South somewhere.'

'Much obliged for the news,' Frank replied with a tip of his hat.

The sheriff did not seem too pleased with Frank's response to the news. 'You don't sound too excited, Frank.'

'The old man wasn't on my list,' Frank noted, moving on.

'That list is a whole lot shorter now, huh?' Sheriff Hancock called after him, steadying himself against a gust of wind. 'Thanks to you and your brothers, Frank.'

Frank Daniels did not bother to look back. It wasn't praise he wanted, but more graves. Three more: Henry Lowe, Gila Murdock and Newson Murdock. That was all he wanted. Leastwise, this was what Marlene Welch contended later as he sat with her in her window, sipping a hot toddy and watching the street.

'So, what is wrong with that?' Frank replied mildly.

'It is fatal, that is what is wrong with it, Frank. Ask Urban and Virgil,' Marlene shot back.

His scowl cut deep.

'Somethin' on your mind, Marlene?' Frank asked.

'Yes, as a matter of fact there is,' she responded with a scowl of her own. 'I don't want you to go. There, I've said it.'

Smoke trickled from Frank's lips as he drew his cigar from his mouth. In the warmth of the barroom, with its drinkers and gamblers, its oil lights and the pleasant tinkle of a piano, his color was becoming good once more. To one woman at least, he was the most impressive man she had ever seen.

'It seems to me we have had this conversation before, Marlene,' he said.

'No,' she replied. 'It is different this time around. When we spoke last time, you had four brothers alive. Now there are only two.'

'Are you blaming me for their deaths?' he asked.

'Urban and Virgil would not be dead if they had not followed you. They would have quit after a few days, like normal men.'

'So, I'm not normal now. Is that it?' he asked.

'I am not goin' to argue with you, Frank,' Marlene argued. Her manner was intense as she leaned forwards. 'But can't you see what you are doin'? You are chasin' something only you want, and the price is far too high. Can't you grasp that before it is too late?'

'No,' he said solemnly. 'I can't.'

Marlene Welch reached out and took his hand,

her heart in her eyes.

'It is not a good time,' was all he said.

'There will never be a better time, Frank. Why do you think I have always loved you but never wanted to marry you?'

'Was it because I never asked,' he grinned, trying to lighten the mood.

'I am being serious, Frank Daniels. If I had wanted to marry you, I would have asked, and I think you know it. I am hardly your dewy-eyed little clingin' vine type, waitin' for her big, brave man to make all the decisions, now am I?'

He conceded the point, but he still did not know what she was driving at.

Marlene Welch explained.

'I am ready to marry you now, Frank,' she said simply. 'Maybe it took you going after those outlaws and riskin' your life to make me see what it would be like if you were dead. I would still be in the same position I am now, you understand? There would still be no other man for me, even if you were in your grave. It is bad enough bein' an old maid, carryin' the torch for somebody that is hardly ever there. But at least you are alive. If you were dead, then I might as well be dead, too. Will you marry me and forget traipsin' around the country tryin' to get yourself killed? Say you will, Frank.'

Frank Daniels' face was pale once more.

'Marlene, I . . . I don't know what to say.'

She hung her head. 'Just say yes.'

He was silent for a long moment, holding both her

hands and gazing into her eyes after she raised her head again.

At last he spoke.

'You are right, Marlene. I have always wanted to marry you. And I guess I was waitin' for you to show me that you would marry me. And we will.' A pause. 'Right after I get back.'

Marlene withdrew her hands quickly. She was close to tears as she got to her feet.

'Because you would rather hate than love, Frank. That is it, isn't it? You love me, but you love what you are doin' more, don't you? You want the whole world to know that nobody can hurt Frank Daniels and get away with it, and you don't care what it costs to prove that point. . . .'

'Marlene, please. . . .'

'Well, now I will tell you why I never begged you to marry me, Frank. It is because I always knew your weakness.'

'Weakness?' Frank looked surprised as he fixed her with a steely stare, looking more than ever like a man without a weakness to his name. 'And what might that be?'

Marlene Welch lifted her chin.

'You don't know when to quit, Frank. Oh, I know others might see that as a virtue. But with you, it goes too far. When you start somethin', you can't quit until you have won. You were always like that. You always thought more of winning and playing the role of Frank Daniels than you did of anything or anyone else. That is what made you go wanderin' when you should have been here with your family. When you should have been settlin' down with me and raisin' kids. Mister, you are just usin' what happened to your mother and now your brothers as an excuse to duck what you are really scared of – bein' ordinary.'

She paused. Frank glowered. Drinkers had fallen silent to listen.

'That is your weakness, Frank Daniels, and I am beggin' you one last time to tell your brothers they can go back home.'

He could not do it.

It was asking too much.

Behind the pile of dry brush near the mouth of the pass, a jackrabbit suddenly stopped grazing and held its foolish head high, long ears pricked, sensitive nose sniffing the hot Indian Nations air. Then it bounded away, thumping the dusty earth with long hind legs and quickly disappearing into the rocks where it was safe.

The sound which frightened the jackrabbit had the opposite effect on the outlaws watching Henry Lowe as his hand hovered above the plunger. They were hidden in a draw off the trail, and they had been waiting for that very sound. If Henry's carefully conceived plan succeeded, and if their nerve did not fail them, they would all be rich men.

Henry Lowe himself had charge of the igniter, although two of his men had placed the dynamite along the trail.

Each month at the same time, the Buffalo Mine

secretly shipped its takings across the Little Dog Plains. Henry had learned of the shipments by accident, during his last journey across the Indian Nations. He had been itching to make his play ever since that time.

This was the big one that he and the gang needed.

Rumbling through the pass came an iron dinosaur on wheels, an armor-plated wagon with four heavily armed outriders and a further four men inside behind the narrow gun ports. It required a team of eight horses to haul the rig, weighed down as it was by a strong box filled with yellow gold and carrying the added weight today of an overweight lawman.

Marshal John Blythe had followed the gang all the way from Wyoming. He was convinced now that the only possible attraction for Henry Lowe on the plains had to be the Buffalo Mine shipment. He had insisted on joining the guard this trip, he and his rifle.

The newspapers that splashed the story of the robbery across the front pages of the West in the days following did not miss the irony of the marshal's death. It seemed to make Henry Lowe and the Murdock Gang's triumph complete.

CHAPTER 14

THE TRAIL EXPLODES

Dust swirled around the three horseback riders as they came out of the draw and cut south. South lay the town of Rinconada Falls on the Sweetwater river – the suspected destination of the men who had plundered the Buffalo Mine gold.

Frank Daniels led the way as always, with Casey next and Hugh bringing up the rear. It was still warm in the Indian Nations, but winter was slowly working its way down the continent. The dust billowed free, but there was a chill in the air despite this, which moved Hugh and Casey to ride in their sheepskins. But not big Frank. He seemed unaware of the chill, or of hunger, or fatigue. To his brothers he was either the craziest man they knew, or the toughest. It had been that way for Frank ever since Mescalero.

Mescalero was the place where they had struck it lucky with a one-time rider of the owlhoot trail named Shoofly Smith. Crippled now and living on charity, Shoofly had a grudge against his former comrades in the Murdock Gang. They had left him to rot years ago after he had been shot up in a train robbery. He had been waiting to get even with them ever since. As a former associate of Henry Lowe's, Shoofly had been questioned several times by the law. His hate for Lowe and the Murdock Gang had never been strong enough to betray him to the law but helping the Daniels brothers was altogether different. They were plain folks, like him. They had a personal grudge, and they plainly meant to see that they settled it.

Shoofly had told them about Rinconada Falls, 'the kind of place even a self-respecting scorpion would dodge'. He had holed up with the gang several times at that remote, little known hell-hole. Rinconada Falls' proximity to the site of the gold robbery was enough to convince Shoofly that this was where Lowe and his gang would be hiding out.

Another twenty miles, and the Daniels would know if the old bad man's theory held water. At nightfall the three brothers had reached the edge of a butte overlooking the tiny settlement on the dusty banks of the Sweetwater river.

Frank slid from his saddle to flex his leg, listening to distant sounds of revelry. A gunshot echoed, followed by faint laughter. There was no guarantee that the gang was there, but to the brothers it sure felt as if they would be.

'I'm goin' down to take a gander,' Frank said, '. . . to see for myself.'

'We should all go, Frank,' Casey said with little conviction. Neither Casey nor Hugh had displayed much enthusiasm for the hunt since leaving Missouri this time. Frank blamed their diminished spirit on one thing – women. Hugh's wife and Lucy Keller had done their damnedest to persuade them not to resume the hunt, and Frank had had his work cut out to convince his brothers to follow him.

Even allowing for the fact that he had never known his brothers altogether that well, Frank was surprised by their lack of resolution. He could not understand how any man could allow Henry Lowe and the Murdock Gang to go unpunished for the crimes and murders they had committed.

'It is easier if I just go alone,' Frank said now. 'Less chance of us bein' spotted.'

Hugh sighed and pushed his hat to the back of his head.

'You'll come back for us if you strike anything, won't you?' he said. 'I mean, you are not gonna take them on singlehanded, are you, Frank?'

'You sound like somebody I know in Blue Springs Creek,' Frank noted with a grunt, breaking open his shotgun to check the loads. He closed the weapon with a snap. 'She thinks I'm doin' this for the glory. Well, I am not. I want them dead, and I can't do it alone.' He nodded. He added another grunt. 'I'll be right back,' he then said.

He walked through darkness, making no sound – which was remarkable for a man of his size. He chose the soft spots to step, and his eyes were never still. There were sentries, he realized, as he closed in from the north side. He read this as rock-solid confirmation that the outlaws were in residence.

Reaching the first decaying buildings, Frank squatted down between a corral and a hen run to study the narrow, rutted track that passed for a main street. He watched a ragged Mexican who appeared to be weeping over a dead burro. His gaze moved to the tumbledown church, squatting incongruously in the very center of the town, facing the saloon. There were broad wooden steps leading up to the front doors, and standing on these were two men. They were laughing. They had pistols in their hands.

Frank Daniels had seen one of them back in Cibola Hills. With Henry Lowe.

The outlaws roared with rude laughter as they fired into the air, and the bigger one began to sing:

'Ah shot a burro.
Ah know not where,
All ah I know is,
He ain't needin' no more air.'

His partner laughed so hard that he staggered down the steps, lost his balance and fell. His gun went off, and there was a clatter of breaking glass from the saloon. A flood of angry outlaws poured into the street at once.

'You brainless idjits!' Frank heard someone yell. 'You could have killed somebody.'

The drunk outlaw was on his knees, still laughing.

'Hey, Newson!' he called to the big man on the steps. 'Sing 'em the song.'

Newson! Frank thought, staring hard at the big man. Newson Murdock. One of the five!

He fingered the black pebbles in his pocket as the wrangle continued. . . .

It had come quickly. He had not really expected to run down the entire gang so easily. Here he was, unseen and unsuspected. Remembering the funeral of his dear mother – remembering Urban, dead and cold on a bluff in the middle of nowhere – remembering Virgil in the little cemetery outside Cibola Hills.

Trail's end.

Frank had to shake his head to clear the bitter memories that clouded his eyes and his judgement. He stared down at his hands. His knuckles were showing white as he gripped the shotgun.

He twitched suddenly at the roar of a gun. Looking up, he saw that the outlaws were terrorizing the Mexican with the dead burro again, pumping slugs over his head and into the dust around him.

And then Henry Lowe appeared.

Any lingering intention Frank Daniels had of reporting back to his brothers vanished in that instance, then and there.

All he had to do was cut loose with the shotgun.

But he didn't move. He had no taste for suicide,

132

and he would be one man against what looked like about twenty outlaws. So his legs would not take him away from Henry Lowe, but his mind would not allow him to invite certain death.

Lowe laughed and rested his hands on his hips. He was amused by the grief and terror of the man with the dead burro, who was now laboriously unbuckling a heavy pack from the dead animal's back.

'What you got there, pard?' he laughed. 'The lost Apache gold, perhaps?'

'Watch out there, Lowe,' Newson Murdock joked. 'He might be reaching for a shootin' iron. . . .'

'A weapon, a weapon!' a bearded, drunken bandit screamed in mock horror, throwing up his hands and falling to his knees. 'God spare us all! Don't shoot, mister, I have got a kid and five wives!'

Outlaws almost fell over laughing at this sally, but the man with the dead burro was shaking with fear.

'Por favor,' he said, 'it is not the weapon, just the dynamite.'

Suddenly everyone stopped laughing.

'Dynamite?' breathed Newson Murdock, the one who had gunned down the burro just for the hell of it. He looked a little pale. 'Are you sayin' your critter was totin' explosives, old man?'

'Yeah,' the towner shrugged. 'That there is Emilio, the powder monkey from the mine. That would be dynamite in them bags, right enough, *señor.*'

'You drunken bums!' Henry Lowe snarled. 'You could have blown us to kingdom come.' He gestured at the Mexican man. 'You. Get that stuff out of here. Move!'

The Mexican fumbled with the pack but his shaking hands would not cooperate. With a curse, Henry Lowe ordered him off and swung on big Newson Murdock.

'Take care of it,' he snapped. 'And don't drop the stuff just because you are drunk.'

As Newson Murdock moved towards the burro, Henry Lowe began to walk away.

In that instant, Frank Daniels came to a decision. Destiny had dealt him a joker, and if he didn't play it, he deserved to lose the game.

Sweeping the shotgun to his shoulder, he emptied both barrels into the bulging leather sack.

Casey Daniels almost fell over with shock as the bellow of the explosion came rocking up the butte. They saw the fireball erupting in the heart of the outlaw town below. The brothers stared down in open-mouthed awe as houses burst into flame and gunfire began to punctuate the screams of the injured.

They exchanged wide-eyed stares. They did not want to go down there. They had prayed that Frank would find Rinconada Falls totally empty of outlaws, but now there was no choice. Frank was down there, on foot and alone.

That had to mean he needed his brothers.

As they mounted and spurred downslope, Frank was fighting for his life. At the crucial moment, his leg had given out on him, slowing his retreat so badly that he had been sighted in the light of the blazing buildings.

He didn't think he had a chance, but he felt damn good, nonetheless. He only had to look over his shoulder to feel even better. The explosion had cut a swathe through the bad men, and many lay dead or dying in the street.

He had had the pure joy of seeing Newson Murdock disintegrate before the eyes, and he delayed just long enough to fling a black stone into the street before taking to his heels.

His pounding heart told him that Henry Lowe might be dead, too. That hope lent him strength as he dragged his game leg after him and ran for . . . for what? There was nothing ahead but the half mile of open country between the town and the river. Behind him, a mob of maddened outlaws were screaming his name.

It was worth dying if he had nailed Henry Lowe, too, he was telling himself, but then he heard the voice: 'Horses, you halfwits! Bring the horses!'

Frank stumbled, slowed dangerously and turned around.

Silhouetted against a blazing barn, Henry Lowe was unmistakable as he waved his muscular arms and shouted with powerful lungs.

'If Daniels gets away, I will skin every mother's son. Horses! Bring me a horse!'

Frank turned his back and kept going, concentrating solely on what speed he could muster with his injured leg.

How in hell had Henry Lowe survived? Had Frank
played the hand wrong? Should he have passed up
the temptation of the dynamite to await his chance
and be sure of Lowe?

Would his brothers finish what he had begun? The
answer had to be no. They did not have the grit for
it. Not like him. They did not hate the way he did,
and he both despised and loved them for that.

His head thudded against his ribcage. He could
hear hoofbeats but would not look back for fear of
losing a few inches of headway.

And then his brothers were there, sweeping
towards him hell for leather.

The pain in his leg was nearly forgotten, and now
he had all the time in the world. He ran and
returned fire and ran again. Two outlaws stumbled as
his brothers opened up, and one of the bad men
went down. The flames from the town were making
the river flats bright as day. Casey shouted Frank's
name and came heeling towards him, while Hugh
slowed the enemy with a sweeping volley of fire from
his repeating rifle.

'Kill him! Kill him!'

It was Henry Lowe's cry, above the gunfire and
roaring flames, Frank braced himself and lifted a
powerful arm. Casey leaned from his saddle, right
arm lowered. The two arms slammed together and
held. Frank kicked high, and the kid swept him
around behind him. Frank's rump hit horsehide in
the same instant that Hugh, horse and all, went down
fifty yards behind him.

The outlaws' howling alerted Frank and Casey, but even as Casey changed direction, it was already too late. A bandit wearing a red Mexican shirt was standing over Hugh, pumping shot after shot into his body.

'Hugh!' Casey screamed, and spurred the horse towards the fallen man. 'Hold on, Hugh!'

'Don't be a fool, kid!' Frank yelled, grabbing for the reins. 'He's dead, and so will we be if we go closer. Right, hard right, kid!'

But Casey, tears streaming down his face, kept the horse running straight ahead until a fist crashed against the side of his jaw and almost knocked him from the saddle. But Frank held on to his youngest brother with one hand and jerked viciously on the right rein with the other. The horse veered sharply, and they lurched away with hot lead following.

Outlined against the yellow fires, dark horsemen followed.

CHAPTER 15

THE AFTERMATH

Casey Daniels winced as Frank put the cold compress against his swollen jaw.

'Hold it there,' Frank growled, and then he abruptly swung away to peer over the rimrock.

Horsemen!

Frank sleeved his sweating face – so Henry Lowe was not quitting. He was following hard with what was left of his outlaw army, leaving the Daniels no time to do anything but run, as they had run for almost twenty-four hours non-stop.

They were headed home.

There was no place else for them, with their hunters herding them away from the towns and main trails, with Frank's leg bleeding and the double-burdened horse almost on its last legs. And the rain kept coming down, as it had been for the past twelve hours, like somebody had busted a pipe in the sky.

'I can hear 'em, Frank,' Casey panted, wide-eyed as Frank swung back to him. 'They are goin' to get us, aren't they? We'll never see home again, and Lucy won't. . . .'

'Stop the bawlin', kid,' Frank ordered.

Casey looked resentful.

'Goin' to die tough? Is that what you aim to do, Frank? You been tough all your life, and now that is all you got. Not a word about poor Hugh or. . . .'

'Mount up, kid,' Frank said flatly. 'We are goin' to make it.'

When they reached the Blue Springs Creek waterway that night, they were barely able to ford it. When the outlaws made to follow them, Frank opened up and sent two of them to a watery grave before Henry Lowe called the rest of his men back.

Frank was able to hold them back for nearly an hour. By then, the creek was up another two feet and plainly impassable.

It was only as they dragged themselves wearily on to the horse for the short ride into town that Casey made a revelation to Frank.

'Frank, I'm hit.'

Frank's face turned pale and his heart sank. 'Hold on, kid.'

On the rain-sodden street, Frank smoked a cigar and leaned on his rifle.

He was all alone.

He stood outside the Bella Union Saloon, where his lone surviving brother lay dying in Marlene

Welch's feathered bed.

The wound that had looked so innocent to the naked eye had proven just the opposite. There was nothing more they could do for young Casey. Even though his younger brother kept calling for him, Frank remained on the street in the cold, the wind and the rain. Waiting. Clicking black pebbles in this hand. Watching with the eyes of a hunter while the eyes of Blue Springs Creek watched him.

They could not understand him. Frank knew. None of them. The sheriff had wired for marshals to search for the outlaw gang, though the old-timers were quite insistent that nobody could cross the creek at its present level.

But Frank Daniels continued to wait for Henry Lowe.

Marlene accused him of hoping the outlaw might find his way across, but Frank denied this. He was a good judge of men, he told himself, and he judged that Henry Lowe could hate every bit as hard as Frank Daniels.

A door creaked open in the wind. Frank turned his head. Marlene stared down at him.

'He's goin' fast, Frank.'

'I can't leave the street,' was all Frank said in response.

Her eyes brimmed with tears.

'Haven't you had enough, Frank? You lost your mother, and now you have sent your four brothers after her! Isn't that enough, even for a man like you?'

They did not understand. No one ever really

understood him, or men like him.

As he made to reply, some sixth sense sent him diving low. The bullet whistled overhead and buried itself in the saloon wall.

'Got him!' croaked Henry Lowe as he staggered forwards on rubbery legs.

Blinking through the rain and deceived by his own exhaustion, the outlaw leader was seeing what he wanted to see – Frank Daniels lying dead.

But Frank was playing possum, and the possum suddenly came back to life. Frank's rifle roared again and again. Henry fell first, and then a hawk-faced gang member after him.

Henry could not believe it. He raised his Colt with a bloodied hand and fired.

But soon the guns fell silent. The outlaws lay side by side, face down in the mud. Frank crossed to them, and his eyes were blazing as he took two black pebbles from his pocket and dropped them in the street.

It was finally over.

Now he was ready for other things: he was now free.

He saw Lucy Keller and Marlene Welch in the saloon doorway as he crossed the street. He could not disguise the spring in his step – but their faces sobered him as he drew closer. As he made to speak, Lucy got in ahead of him.

'It is too late, Frank. Casey is dead.'

The girl turned inside, and Marlene followed her.

'It was always too late, Frank,' she said, and then

she was gone, gone in a way she would never have gone from him before. Gone, he knew with sudden searing clarity, she was gone forever from him.

Frank Daniels stepped back into the rain. He did not want to see the face of another dead brother. He was feeling already what his hatred had not allowed him to feel before.

There was no sign now of the people who had cheered him in the past. Frank and two dead men had the street to themselves.

The doors of the town were closed, its windows empty. Frank Daniels had what he wanted. Now he had to learn to live with it.

Forever.

Now he knew he should have married Marlene Welch when he had had the chance.

But Frank Daniels would have to continue to be who he was.

CHAPTER 16

THE COURT OF COMMON SENSE

Six months later. . .

'They've caught the fellow who stole Ben Allridge's horse!'

The cry carried from claim to claim, and sweating miners tossed aside shovel and pan, stopped a moment to consider the news, and drifted toward the main camp.

Frank Daniels stirred. His massive frame stretched comfortably in the shade of his tent, a favorite position in the later afternoon while other men labored.

'Ben Allridge's a fool and his horse is an ass,' Frank said indignantly, and the saying of it made him feel better – not really, as nothing made him forget the pain of the deaths of his brothers – but it helped greatly to break the spell cast over him by the memories of his lost love, too: Marlene Welch.

143

Frank had hoped that once he had eliminated Henry Lowe and his gang, he and Marlene would wed, and he would settle down. But that had not been the case.

Frank sighed. He got to his feet, stretched more, and brushed aimlessly at his clothing. He then bent to flick at the dust layering his tightly tailored boot. Big and sun-whipped from his recent journeys, Frank still held the touch of pallor across his features which hinted at the time he had spent recovering from the bullet wound in his leg.

He had never admitted how much he loved Marlene Welch – though that no longer mattered, as his hunt of Henry Lowe and the Murdock Gang had cost him all.

Inside his patchwork shanty of canvas and board, Frank donned a ruffled shirt and cravat, a waistcoat of calfskin, and a frock coat cut high in the back with fine buttons and wide silk lapels. It was not his usual style. The coat alone had cost him fifty dollars. On his head he cocked his dirty and worn old hat.

He had acted like a crazed fool after the deaths of his brothers. In six months he had gotten drunk, gambled and spent like a madman with nothing to lose.

Maybe he didn't have anything to lose.

Forty men milled like nervous cattle in the opening before the circular tent saloon. Tied soundly to the trunk of a tree was a young miner known to Frank as John Bishop.

Upon Frank's approach, the talk and milling came to a stop. Had Judge Glenn Conley, on his bench back in New York or wherever he was from back East, viewed the scene, he might well have experienced a momentary lessening of hostility toward a man like Frank. On the other occasion that Judge Conley had held 'court' in this Colorado mining camp, belligerent crowds had sensed the edge of calm reason in his rulings and noted favorably his judicial bearing. Conley nodded to the many around and stood silent. The assemblage must act of its own accord, in the terms and traditions of the ancient folkmoot that ruled in the gold camp.

Ben Allridge finally spoke up in a shrill voice that betrayed his emotion. 'I want this horse thief declared guilty, so I can string him up.' His declaration was promptly followed by sufficient eyes to make the comment popular amongst the crowd.

Frank, acting as a sort of bailiff, cleared his throat portentously. 'The court,' he said, 'is in order.'

He walked to the tree and gazed solemnly at John Bishop. John was a young, fiery-eyed man of bullish strength and a reputation for sudden violence. In his youthful appearance he reminded Frank of Casey. John spat contemptuously at Frank's ruffled shirt front, but Frank craftily side-stepped without losing his composure. Turning away, he nodded to Judge Conley.

The judge then said, 'All right, Mr Allridge. What's the story?'

'I caught him in the very act, Judge,' Ben Allridge

said heatedly. 'Got a touch of the sun, so I rode in early from the claim. Left the horse saddled and tied while I went into the tent to rest. Came out later to find John Bishop riding off on my horse.'

There was an angry murmur from the others. 'Go on, Mr Allridge,' Judge Conley said, 'when it gets quiet, that is.'

'I hollered and John started kicking the horse to get him going,' said Ben. 'Then the Wilson brothers ran up and caught him and brought him back and we tied him up after some fancy scufflin'.'

Frank's gaze found the Wilson brothers – Donovan and Daniel – in the crowd. They both nodded vigorously in agreement, and the older of the two, Donovan, said, 'It's what happened, Judge . . . Frank.'

'I wouldn't take three hundred dollars for that horse,' Ben Allridge declared. 'A good mount's scarce in these parts, and there's none I've seen as good as that one.'

Frank took a visual cue from Judge Conley and acted as his voice, looking at John Bishop. 'If you've got any defense, John, you'd best tell the court.'

'I've been associating with polecats so long I got lonesome for a horse,' John Bishop fired back.

Looking to the judge again and receiving the nod, Frank said, 'Maybe you were drunk?'

'I was sober,' protested John.

As Frank went to speak, Judge Conley decided to finally speak up first. 'Maybe you were just claim-happy, Mr Bishop. Sort of lost your head for a minute.'

'Nah, most sensible thing I've done since I got to this hell-hole gold country,' John Bishop retorted, 'I'd have ridden that horse straight to Santa Fe and points east.'

'He's a confessed horse thief,' Ben Allridge said, high and angry.

'Seems like time for a hangin',' Donovan Wilson chimed in.

Frank sighed and waited for the judge to make his declaration. 'There being no defense, John Bishop is found guilty of attempting to steal a horse of Ben Allridge. Now there is the question of penalty.'

'He's guilty, he hangs,' said Allridge.

Frank turned on him and stared coldly. 'The judge here is the elected presiding officer of this meeting, and he will do the fair thing according to common sense.'

'You afraid to hang a horse thief, Frank?' Ben Allridge asked.

'John did a fool thing,' Frank said, 'which I don't think he'll likely repeat. And you've still got your horse, Ben.'

Allridge turned to the judge. 'Ain't you goin' to hang him?'

Frank felt a wave of distaste rise in him for Ben Allridge: a man wronged but claiming compensation to the hilt – the compensation of another man's life.

It was then that Judge Glenn Conley declared: 'John Bishop gets forty lashes on his back for temporarily losing his head and trying to ride off on another man's horse.'

'I'll be shot!' Ben Allridge yelled. 'Of all the cowardly. . . .'

'While the Wilson brothers turn John around at his tree there and deliver the sentence,' Frank cut in, 'I'm goin' to ask the judge's permission to lick Ben Allridge for calling him a coward.'

Ben Allridge's eyes widened. The judge nodded his head and said, 'Court's adjourned.'

CHAPTER 17

CURTAIN CALL

The following morning was grey and cold as Frank walked north. If there was a stiffer man in the Mother Lode, he was not sober to suffer as Frank Daniels did. His arms and legs, especially the one he'd received a bullet in about six months ago, ached sorely, and his head seemed split and held together only by the bandage bound tightly over his brow. One eye was purple, puffed and closed, and his lower lip felt like some frog sat there. His nose was broken fearsomely, and he groaned as the chill air buffed it.

When the first ray of light topped a craggy peak, Frank stopped beside a stream to bathe his face. He sat awhile to rest and cast a suspicious eye on his companion.

John Bishop knelt down like a very old man to cup his hands and drink at the stream. When he stood up, Frank could see the pain in the deeply drawn lines around his mouth. Frank could imagine the striated back shorn of flesh and stiffening in the cold. John was like some thick trunk of tree bitten cruelly by the axe.

'You should have stole a horse instead of tanglin' with Ben Allridge,' John said to Frank. 'They beat my hide off, but I still got my beautiful face.'

Frank grunted. 'Ben's in poor shape this morning, too,' he said.

John Bishop nodded. 'You was doing fine till the two of you went twenty feet down that coyote shaft.'

Frank winced at the recollection of that plunge, the rock sides of the shaft burning his hide raw and the slag heap landing that came near to unhinging him.

'You've busted me up for fair, John,' Frank said accusingly. 'I was a respected man once . . . with a mother and a nice lady who loved me, and brothers who worshipped me, and respected here in the community till you stole that nag and I got mad at Ben Allridge as he demanded that we hang you.'

'You've got a fair, sensible streak in you or I'd be danglin' from a tree this very minute,' John said.

Frank shook his head, and then hung on to it a moment with both hands to stop the throbbing. 'They don't want a bailiff that doesn't want to hang a horse thief. That's why I was told to git when they dragged me from that hole.'

'Thing is, I ain't a real horse thief,' said John. 'You got a mind and could see it. You're a man of justice. . . .'

'Justice ... justice can cost a man everything,' Frank replied. 'And you would have done until a real horse thief came along.' He got to his feet, rolled a little with his dizziness, and then started north.

From Mt Bullion, to Bear Valley, to Bagby, to Coulterville and on north he marched in the coming days. And it was a painful journey to a man of pride. Frank felt the deep pity for himself – a man without his parents, without a woman to love, and without his brothers: that's what he was now – a man alone.

He looked the odd figure in rough pants and jacket cast off by some camp along the way; a filthy flop-brimmed hat partially obscuring a battered face thick matted with a tawny beard.

The two found refuge in a lonely Sierra camp. Though most in the camp wanted to sing and dance around the fires, Frank had one single drink and brooded in the shadows.

Next morning he pushed on again, and behind him labored John Bishop. John had been beaten too, and driven out, but was not broken. 'You're a man of justice, Frank,' he would say.

But Frank Daniels knew that this was not so. He knew he had acted outside the law when he hunted Henry Lowe and the Murlock Gang, killing nearly every last one of them at the cost of his brothers' lives.

The Dramatic Hall at the camp of Hogleg had a low ceiling, with a slab-timbered roof that tilted south to shed the rains, and a rough board floor that tilted north to shed tobacco juice and the tears that flowed copiously on nights of rich drama. The slightly elevated stage rested precariously on wooden horses, and a painted female figure of some bosomy munificence graced the calico curtains that drew the thin line between audience and player.

Hogleg was a larger camp than Mariposa, and to John Bishop's practised eye, even less well organized. It had the feel of an ornery, brawling camp, and John was surprised that Frank would linger there. And he was purely astonished when, on the third day, Frank filed a small pan and shovel claim on a stream a mile out of camp, and on that Saturday night followed other citizens of the camp to the Dramatic Hall.

Booming laughter, oaths and gunfire collided mightily with wind bolts from tall mountain peaks as miners crowded toward the hall. A large, soiled banner, pummeled by the gusts, proclaimed:

THE GLOVERS
LOVELY MARLENE AND GRAND WINFIELD
WITH COMPANY
IN
LADY OF LYONS AND *OTHELLO*

Frank sat well back in the hall, a curious sickness in him, the like of which assailed him at curtain time. Marlene had drawn him here, even in his present sorry condition – and Grand Winfield, the man who'd married the love of Frank Daniels' life.

Marlene's round, full voice jerked Frank back into

the present. He was on his feet and roaring with the rest when she took the stage. He'd seen her perform numerous times – as a dancer, and in burlesque and other performances – and still she took his breath away. Her little speech was mainly cut off, and she just stood there smiling and inclining her head, and sweet-looking enough to squeeze a man's heart.

She raised her hands finally. 'The show's on,' Marlene called out, 'and we'll do our best for you handsome gentlemen. We've only one request – no shooting till the final curtain!'

The clamor rose again, and Frank blessed the anonymity of his hat, beard and battered face – for Marlene was close in that little hall: too close, and he felt like a sad dog of a man.

The evening sped by while Frank dreamed, and Marlene and Winfield spun their magic for lonely gold seekers. It was near the end of the program when Frank made his grievous error. Grand Winfield, fortifying himself between scenes with hot water and whiskey, had overdone it and become befuddled. When he labored to a tortuous halt in mid-speech, Frank from far back in the hall intoned, '. . . then must you speak, of one that loved not wisely but too well. . . .'

Winfield Glover snorted dead center, swung around and stared. Frank struggled to his feet in confusion and scuffled out into the windy night.

Frank squatted three hours next morning over the streambed and panned a lucky ounce of gold and was ignorant of just when John Bishop arrived to sit

153

in the tree shade and smoke and contemplate him.

'You know them Glovers, don't you, Frank?' John said finally. Frank nodded, sifting rhythmically at his pan.

'I figured so,' said John. 'Else why do we stop here and file a claim and go down to a showing at the Dramatic Hall. . . .'

'I stop here,' replied Frank shortly. 'You can go where you please, John.'

'Why do you keep hid under your hat and bush whiskers, Frank? You afraid of her?'

Frank stopped his sifting. He set the pan down on a rock and looked over at his companion. John, in some special way, had become a part of Frank during their long trek north on the Mother Lode. He'd become an honest, dogged, goading presence who reminded him of his brothers – especially Casey – and who at first had followed and had later driven Frank, like a conscience. He was prodding now – but too hard.

'You think too much, John Bishop. Either pan gold or get out.'

'The girl's in trouble, Frank. Her and that man of hers are in a claim fight with a dude named Rush Fetters. He's about to beat them out.'

Frank picked up his pan again and resumed sifting.

'It's an odd point,' John went on. 'Rush was working quartz ledges on both sides of a little gulch. The Grand Glover tracked a rich placer run in the stream between the ledges and claimed it. Fetters raised hell, of course, and some of the boys think he's mean, but in his rights. Most don't give a hoot, to be honest.'

'I don't give a hoot either,' Frank shot back.

'They say Marlene Glover brought the husband into the gold camps because the stage was killin' him off. They say if Rush takes this strike away from him, it will kill him, sure as I am sitting in this shade. Don't seem just, somehow.'

'Hold court and settle it then,' Frank snapped.

John got up and knocked the ashes from his pipe. 'They are holding court tomorrow night, and Rush is already spending the gold he's gonna be awarded.'

Frank sifted on, head bowed, still searching his pan for the tell-tale glitter. He was mightily relieved when John Bishop walked away.

CHAPTER 18

LOVE AND THE
LAW IN HOGLEG

'It is not in my heart to dispossess a lady of such charm as Mrs Glover of any rightful claim she may have on a fortune to match her rising fame,' Rush Fetters was saying smoothly. The late afternoon sun struck a lively gleam in Rush's over-large black eyes and broad, toothy smile. He was a big man sure in the knowledge of his shrewdness and arresting good looks.

'This matter of a placer strike her and her husband made directly in the midst of my quartz ledges can be easily resolved,' Rush added.

The men of Hogleg stirred and nodded to one another, and Jed Agler, the presiding officer, looked hugely comforted. To be caught in the middle of a dispute between the adroit and sinister Rush Fetters and a purposeful husband and wife team like the Glovers was neither pleasant nor healthful. Jed was a simple and honest man who was well aware that a wrong move could ruin him.

Winfield Glover, from across the circle of men, cleared his throat. 'What is your purpose, sir – your offer?' he said in a half whisper.

Rush shrugged, gesturing in comic exaggeration with his large, flat hands. 'I would like to marry Mrs Glover!'

The miners howled with raucous laughter. They pounded knees, slapped hats to the earth and jig stepped. And Rush Fetters grinned immensely.

'It is the only answer,' one man roared rather loudly. 'Marry 'em up, Jed!'

Winfield Glover crossed the space in three short jumps. His nose collided agonizingly with Rush Fetter's suddenly doubled fist. He shuddered, groaned aloud and fell face-forward. Marlene Welch was down beside him swiftly, while Jed Agler took out his gun and fired twice in the air to restore order.

The sight of the girl ministering to the fallen Glover sobered the men of Hogleg more effectively than Agler's gunfire. Fun and hell are fine, but no lady is treated like that.

From the very midst of the crowd suddenly stepped a newcomer to camp, holding up his hands, demanding attention. John Bishop, a flushed and angry man, addressed Jed Agler.

'There is a gent here who can talk on this case,' he said loudly. 'He is a man born with a nugget of sense

– which is worth more than all the gold we will dig out of this hell-hole. I demand he be heard. I refer to my partner standing right over there.'

Faces turned toward big Frank Daniels, and a path opened to where he stood. Nervously, Frank pulled his hat brim low and straightened his shoulders. He was painfully conscious of Marlene, still kneeling beside Winfield Glover, but looking intently at him. This was a shameful entrance being forced upon him by the treacherous but well-meaning John Bishop.

'Frank Daniels!' John Bishop announced, burning all bridges behind him.

Jed Agler sought to assess Frank. 'You know about this dispute – Mr Daniels?' he said cautiously.

Frank nodded. There was the light now of recognition in Marlene Welch's eyes, her mouth opening slowly in disbelief. And there was finally an urgent and troubling cue for action. Marlene's cue pierced a wave of fright and dread such as Frank had never experienced before. He knew the sorry spectacle he must look, but there was no place to run or hide.

'Hogleg is a fair and just camp,' he managed to say, pulling his eyes from Marlene's. His mind reached back feverishly into his considerations of the sleepless night before. He had gone over John Bishop's account of this dispute minutely, and somewhere he had caught a spark of light.

'It has been held in other camps that according to common sense, gold digging is a franchise from the government, free to all,' he said.

Frank paused to look around, let his words sink in,

158

to build some impact on the crowd. 'If Rush Fetters staked a claim on quartz ledges, let him use that placer claim.'

There was a murmur and shuffling of feet among the miners. They were ripe now for any fair way out. The girl kneeling down by her husband was a plumb embarrassing sight to men instinctively chivalrous; and then, too, this new fellow was talking sense.

'I say this,' said Frank, warming to his subject, 'if in that same gulch of Rush Fetters and Winfield Glover I find a breeze and stake a claim on that breeze and strain gold from it, it is against all comers.'

The final point immensely amused and appealed to the men of Hogleg. They forthwith and loudly voted sanction of Winfield Glover's placer claim and hauled him victoriously to the tent saloon for purposes of vigorous revival. Jed Agler shouted, 'The dispute's settled,' and led the way.

But Rush Fetters stayed behind. He intercepted Frank Daniels on the way out of camp and drew a long knife with fast and deadly purpose – but he never got to use it. Frank Daniels' fist, from out of nowhere, nearly pulverized an ear and drove him senseless to the ground.

'The law is good, and it has to be followed, Rush,' said Frank, grinning and rubbing at his big knuckles. Then he noticed the girl and promptly hustled toward the gathering where Winfield Glover's wits were being joyously resurrected.

But Marlene Welch said, 'Frank Daniels, as I live and breathe!' And there was a tender mockery in her eyes as she hurried toward him, which purely captured Frank Daniels.

'I love you, Marlene,' he said.

She hugged him tighter, and tears dribbled from her eyes. 'I know, you big fool! I love you, too!'